GOD TRIALS

GOD TRIALS

WEREWITCH™ BOOK SEVEN

RENÉE JAGGÉR

LMBPN Publishing
PMB 196, 2540 South Maryland Pkwy
Las Vegas, NV 89109

First US Release, October 2020
eBook ISBN: 978-1-64971-210-3
Print ISBN: 978-1-64971-211-0

"For fuck's sake," Bailey Nordin grumbled, "just give it up. You're never gonna beat me."

A Camaro cruised down the winding country roads in the semi-flat land to the east of Greenhearth, Oregon, driving faster than was smart (or legal), with another car hugging its rear bumper.

The Camaro was glossy black and modified in important ways. It was lowered, for one thing, and had been fitted with a 351 small-block Ford engine.

The vehicle right behind it was a white Audi TT, supercharged. Its exact position varied, but it stayed close behind the Camaro, trying to force it aside and pull ahead.

The driver of the black vehicle had no intention of allowing that to happen.

She pressed her booted foot down harder on the gas, kicking her speed up to a semi-dangerous level as the road ahead began to curve. They were veering northward now, ascending into the mountains, where the terrain would become more treacherous.

The Camaro scythed around the bend, flying far enough out to the side that the driver of the Audi might have been able to pass her if he'd reacted quickly enough. He missed his opportunity, and Bailey rocketed ahead again, barely cutting him off as the road twisted around a low cliff.

A rusty pickup truck rumbled into sight, and the stunned redneck driver laid on his horn in terror as the two sports cars jetted past him and vanished up the mountainside.

Bailey grinned at the white car hovering behind her shoulder, filling her rearview mirror. Its driver was glaring through the windshield. In addition to being out in front, she had one other advantage; she knew this road. He'd never driven on it before.

She tapped her brakes, slowing down a hair, right before they came to a sharp bend, so she was able to coast around the curve with her foot off the gas. The Audi accelerated as soon as Bailey's brake lights went out, only to hit the curve and brake in panicked alarm. Now three car lengths ahead of him, it occurred to her that he might have gone off the road and plummeted into the gorge below.

If that had happened, she had ways of stopping it.

The white car advanced again, though, and its nose was practically touching her bumper once more when the broad pull-over area by the scenic overlook hove into sight. Bailey jerked the wheel to the right and skidded onto the unpaved space less than a second before her opponent.

"Hah!" She laughed as the Camaro fishtailed its way to a stop. "I win." She killed the engine and climbed out as the Audi came to a stop alongside her.

The driver's side door of the white car opened and out stepped a slender, handsome blond man. "Goddammit!" he exclaimed, "I was *this close* to winning, but noooo, you had to go and ruin my first circuit race in this lovely vehicle. Buncha horseshit." He pretended to glare at her.

Bailey put her hands on her hips. "Psshht, yeah, yeah, whatever. I beat your ass fair and square."

He sulked, his mouth pouting and his foot tapping on the pavement.

"So," Bailey went on, "since you lost, you have to forfeit something. That's the way the game is played. Any ideas?"

"Hmm…" He tapped his chin with a long finger. "None whatsoever."

Shaking her head in mild exasperation, Bailey strode over to the wizard, put a hand on his neck, and snagged a quick kiss.

"There," she said. "I'll take that. Fair?"

He rolled his eyes up as though thinking it over. "Sure, why not?"

The two of them leaned against his car, their arms twined around one another's waists, and stared out over the scenic overlook, admiring the hills and gorges and the distant blue peaks of the eastern Cascades.

The werewitch nudged her boyfriend in the ribs. "It was a good race. I kinda figured I'd walk all over you and it'd take you five minutes to catch up after I arrived here, so good job."

"Gosh, thanks." He snorted, but then nuzzled the top of her head. "It *was* a good race. And it's a nice day. The mountains are warmer and drier than how I remember summers in Seattle."

Unspoken but on both of their minds was the question of whether Roland would ever go home, or if he meant to live with Bailey indefinitely in her hometown of Greenhearth. She suspected the latter.

"Yeah," Bailey remarked. "We mostly get Pacific Northwest weather out here, but not quite the same as up by the Puget Sound. Anyway, I'm glad we've got our lives back. Having time to do fun stuff, not always being at war."

Roland nodded. "Indeed." He peered at her face curiously. "Well, as much as things can be 'normal' with you being a *goddess*. That kinda puts a different spin on, uh, *everything*."

She frowned. "I suppose. I'm still me. Most of the time, I don't feel much different, though at times I feel...manic? Like I'm gonna burst or something, not necessarily in a bad way. But you're right. Shit," she muttered and shook her head as she looked back the way they'd come, toward the Hearth Valley.

"I gotta admit," she went on, "I'm still not sure what the hell that means. What the implications are for the future. At least things have been quiet."

Roland gave her hand a squeeze. "In a way, I suppose the whole 'deity' thing is contributing to the quietness. The you-know-who seem to have learned their lesson about fucking with you, and with them out of the way, the impression I'm getting is that relations between witches and Weres have never been better. And not only between us, of course."

She flicked at his face. "I know that, you dork, but yeah, true. All the fight seems to have gone out of the Venatori now that their nasty stuck-up goddess is dead.

Since Bailey defeated Aradia and her elite contingent of witch-knights, the dreaded Venatori Order had been huddled up in Europe, not making a peep. The girl suspected they were too prideful to make a proper peace offering, let alone an apology, and too weakened to offer further retaliation. They probably hoped Bailey would simply forget about them while they licked their wounds.

She hadn't forgotten. She wasn't going to exceed the mandate of self-defense by stamping out their cowering survivors, either, though she had the power to do so. She wasn't like that.

The Men in Black, the Agency, or whatever they were truly called, had also left her alone. They'd worked together against the Venatori, but *not* hearing from them was probably for the best. No news was good news.

"In fact," Bailey added, "I've even had time to do my proper shaman duties, finally. Kinda nice to use my powers for something other than fighting, weird as that might sound coming from me."

"It *does* sound weird," Roland quipped.

In the five weeks since the final battle, she'd ministered to her packs, resolved minor disputes, and helped a pack from southern Oregon sort through a succession crisis. Their alpha was getting old, and too many of his lieutenants wanted to replace him. Bailey had advised them to select the most prudent and thoughtful of the candidates while assuring the others that they would retain positions of honor at the new alpha's right hand.

She'd also abused her cosmic powers *slightly* to make sure Roland got the Audi at an unusually modest price. She was trying to keep to a vow to avoid shit like that, though.

"But," the werewitch opined, "I don't think it'll stay like this forever. Will it? There's always one thing or another about to go wrong. I dunno. Just a hunch."

Roland raised an index finger to his lips. "Shhh. If you absolutely have to worry, don't do it out loud. It can summon the very trouble you're trying to avoid if you're not careful."

Bailey snorted and ruffled his hair. "Bullshit. Old wives' tale. I'll worry as much as I damn well please."

Three seconds after she'd said that, a glowing portal that shimmered like iridescent purple water opened in the air beside them, and out stepped a tall, broad-shouldered man wearing a bulky hooded coat despite the warmth of the day.

Roland cleared his throat. "See? I told you."

Bailey made a point of ignoring the wizard. "Fenris. Hi, haven't seen you in a while. What brings you to, uh, this random stretch of back-ass road?"

As usual, the wolf-god's face was grim but not unfriendly. "Several things," he began in his deep, gravelly voice. "First of all, I'd like to congratulate you on all the progress you've made and the things you've accomplished of late. Routine shaman duties may be less flashy than winning battles against a powerful enemy, but they are no less important. Small problems within the werewolf community can easily grow into *large* problems if not handled with both speed and wisdom."

She smiled. "Thanks."

"But," Fenris continued, drawing himself up.

Roland interrupted, "I *knew* there would be a 'but.'

Speaking of which, bend over and spread 'em, because I'm sure it'll be bad news. Right?"

Fenris glanced at the wizard, grimacing, but did not respond. He looked back at Bailey and resumed his speech.

"But with your recent elevation in power to the level of outright divinity, another issue has presented itself. You have the abilities and potential of a goddess, yet you are not one. At least, not officially. You have no place in the existing pantheon. No one acknowledges you as ruler over anything besides a handful of your friends and supporters."

Bailey blinked. She hadn't thought about it that way.

"And," the wolf-deity went on, "once again, you have more power than you know what to do with, more than you know how to use. In a way, it's like when you first arose as a werewitch months ago. The vast majority of mortals do not become gods. You were born mortal, and your mind is only capable of processing information in a mortal way. So far, anyway."

Roland had slipped out of his casually cocky demeanor and had instead grown aloof with thoughtfulness. "Yes," he agreed. "There are stories of individuals who've suddenly come into immense stores of magical power and found themselves overwhelmed or squandered their potential because they didn't know what the hell they were doing. It probably helps that Bailey has *already* been through that process, sorta, but ascending to godhood is beyond anything I'm familiar with."

The girl looked at the two of them. "I feel fine most of the time, honestly. Once in a while, it's like something surges up inside me, and I'll admit I've been anxious about the whole thing. But so far, it hasn't been a disaster for me. Or anyone else."

Fenris gave a slow nod. "So far, yes. You still possess a mortal body, and you've not exercised the full extent of your powers, which is for the best. If you'd tried, the results might have been devastating. There's no way a mortal can deal with such a change to the fundamental nature of their being without learning some major adaptations, and those changes might permanently alter you."

The werewitch went cold within. She had proven her bravery many times, but being brave was not the same thing as never feeling fear.

Roland sighed. "I can see where this is going. Back to the Other for oodles more training, am I right?"

Fenris's mouth twisted into a small smile. "Not quite."

Bailey took a deep breath. Although things had been nice and quiet for weeks, she'd expected something like this. Though she'd rather linger around town, enjoying the peace she and her allies had purchased through so much effort and sacrifice, rational thought told her that Fenris was right.

What if the Venatori came back, or a disgruntled shaman challenged her, or a natural disaster struck? Bailey might need her new powers, and, not knowing how to fully control them yet, might make a catastrophic mistake, destroying herself or others.

She let out the breath she'd taken. "All right. Whatever I need to do, I'll do it. I've made it through do-or-die scenarios before. Just give me a warning of what to expect. Otherwise, I trust you to teach me. You've always been good at that, Fenris. I could never have got this far without you."

He raised a hand and put it on her shoulder, but then retracted it.

"It is possible," he stated, "that I alone will not be responsible for what is to come next. You see, what I must do is take you before a conclave of other gods and goddesses to discuss with them how to handle your situation. And since I've heard from them only recently, we must go as soon as possible."

Roland squinted. "Which gods are we talking about here? We've met Freya and Balder. Freya is technically my goddess, anyway."

"You, Roland," Fenris answered him, "must stay behind. The deities need to speak to Bailey alone. Or Bailey and me, in any event. At this very moment, they are discussing her. I'll not have her misrepresented."

The werewitch rubbed her eyes. "Okay, then let's go. I'm ready."

Fenris closed the portal he'd arrived through and opened another. Bailey wondered where it led. "I cannot promise you'll be back any particular time."

"Understood." She turned to Roland and clasped him in a big hug. "Take care of my dumbass brothers while I'm gone. Maybe it's them who should be taking care of your dumb ass. Either way. I'll be back when I can, or at least send word."

He kissed the top of her head. "I'll miss you. Stay safe and be strong. You always do, but still."

She kissed him back, then turned toward the glimmering amethyst doorway. "This time, there's no external threat. That helps." She strode into the portal behind the wolf-father, leaving the wizard alone.

He watched her go, trying not to admit that the sight depressed him. A thought popped into his head.

"Oh, shit," he rasped. "What the hell am I supposed to do with her fucking car?"

Bailey's eyes bugged out when she examined the place into which they'd warped. "Holy crap."

"Exactly," Fenris agreed.

The girl let out a sputtering chortle. "I keep forgetting that you've learned how to make jokes. No offense."

After the deep chill and brief sensation of dizziness that always accompanied teleportation, they had emerged into a long, broad, high-ceilinged hall made of pale stone and sparkling blue crystal. Ahead, an arched doorway waited, though a whitish haze obscured what lay beyond it.

"Are we in the Other?" Bailey asked. "Or somewhere else?"

Fenris motioned for her to follow him as he tramped down the hall. "We are in a portion of the divine realm that abuts and overlaps part of the Other. I cannot explain it to you beyond that."

She shrugged. "That'll do. I get the idea."

The corridor looked as though it stretched for miles, but it felt like mere seconds before they passed through the hazy white arch. The room beyond was even more stunning.

The floor and walls were of smooth white marble,

though the windows that looked out on the azure void and clouds were made of thin sheets of the blue crystal they'd seen in the hall. The domed ceiling was marble and gold. Six golden thrones lined the edges of the circular chamber, and everything was studded with jewels that pulsed with an inner light. Everything was so beautiful, it hurt Bailey's eyes to look upon it.

It was the beings seated upon the half-dozen thrones who commanded the most attention.

In the leftmost chair was Freya, whom Bailey recognized, a tall, severely beautiful woman with Nordic features wearing a crown of green leaves and ivy, with emerald sparks playing about her eyes and fingers.

Two seats to the right was Balder, still wearing a golden suit of armor. His hair matched, and his perfectly sculpted face was placid and innocent.

Between the two of them was another Norse deity Bailey assumed must be Thor Odinson, given his huge muscles, red beard, and dented iron helm. A great hammer rested near his booted feet.

To Balder's right was a slender, dark-haired, plainly dressed man Bailey thought looked oddly familiar, though she couldn't think of where she might have seen him or who he might be. He wore a curious, mischievous little smile.

Next in line was a tall, dark-skinned man with a wise, lined, solemn face. He wore a headdress resembling an exotic bird—an ibis?—and a knee-length white sarong-like garment held up by a belt studded with blue, red, and green gems.

Finally, at the far right of the semicircular arrangement

sat a being who looked *mostly* human but had distinctly canine or lupine features, notably his pointed ears and elongated snout. There was gray fur on the backs of his hands, his shoulders, and his feet. Bailey's first impression was that he was a Were caught in the middle of shifting from humanoid to wolf form, but she realized that was incorrect. The figure resembled a dog or a coyote more than a wolf. His face was both playful and weary.

The six deities had been talking among themselves in low, hurried tones, but when Fenris and Bailey intruded, they all looked up in unison.

The red-bearded giant let out a hearty laugh. "Bailey Nordin! We have heard stories about you, girl. Fine tales they were, too. Welcome!"

"Hi," she replied, waving and feeling awkward. Freya and Balder both stared at her in a neutral, reticent fashion, and neither spoke.

The fourth of the Norse deities, the smirking dark-haired fellow, gave her a curt nod. Bailey remembered who he was—the head of the small library in Seattle to which Roland had taken her to test her magical potential many weeks ago. She'd known that the man was more than he seemed, but it had never occurred to her that he was a god.

Fenris extended a hand. "The council. Among my family, you've already met Freya and Balder. This, as you might have guessed, is Thor. And this is my father, Loki."

The girl must have failed to hide her surprise since Loki chuckled faintly as he watched her face. The seated deity looked younger than Fenris did and bore little resemblance to him. He gave a subtle nod, but Bailey couldn't tell if it was directed at her or at his son.

Fenris turned to the two thrones to the right. "And these are Thoth, the Egyptian god of magic and wisdom, and Coyote, the indigenous American trickster-deity whose portfolio also includes the domain of magic."

So does Freya's, Bailey recalled. That must have been what had drawn this motley band together—that, and the fact that more than half of them were related.

Thoth leaned forward. "Greetings. As Thor mentioned, we have heard of you, Bailey. Your career has been most interesting." His voice was low and dry, aged but authoritative.

Coyote, too, peered at her with intense curiosity. "Yes, yes. It's been a long time while we've seen anything like you. These are fascinating times."

All the deities studied the girl for a moment. Freya spoke at last.

"It is good," she stated, "that you have joined us. It will simplify matters a great deal."

Her tone was a bit frosty but not hostile. Both times Bailey had previously encountered the Lady of Witchcraft, she'd been less than friendly, but she had helped her and Roland. She seemed to have the best interests of witchdom at heart.

The girl wasn't sure what the gods wanted of her, or if she was supposed to do anything, so she defaulted to the kind of thing a mortal would think of. She made a joke.

"So, when do I get a chair?" she asked, gesturing at the golden thrones.

Thor chuckled, but the other deities remained stone-faced. Behind her, Fenris coughed and bowed his head.

Freya leaned forward in her seat. "You presume much," she commented.

Fenris replied, "She has only come to—"

"*Silence*," Freya snapped, cutting him off. "Did we invite her here today? Did we ask you to fetch her for us? You do not sit on this council, but you've brought her here of your own free will, without asking us."

Bailey could feel her mentor's tension rising. He and Freya had come to a truce of sorts not long ago, but clearly, it was an unsteady one.

"You," said Fenris, "were discussing her fate based on what you *presume* her next moves would be. I thought it would be useful to ask her those questions in person."

Thoth spoke next, and his tone was calmer than Freya's. "So we shall," he intoned.

The Lady of Sorcery took the floor again. "Bailey Nordin, know this. You have recently acquired the power of a goddess, but that does not make you one of us, any more than a child who looks like her mother *is* her mother. Do not leap to any conclusions as to why we are interested in you."

None of the other deities spoke, but they didn't challenge or disagree with Freya, either.

Balder smiled in his boyish, innocuous way. "You must prove yourself *worthy* of your power, Bailey. We do not know if you will fail to control it and destroy yourself, which could cause great harm to everyone and everything around you."

"Yes," Freya agreed, "and if it reaches that point—if we have reason to believe your new abilities constitute an uncontrollable danger to your world's stability—we shall not hesitate to intervene. We will siphon the power from you and disperse it or dispose of it as we see fit."

Bailey froze, her mouth hanging open, and her heart palpitating in anger, anxiety, and the simple hurt of rejection.

"What, are you threatening me?" she inquired.

Coyote held up a furred hand for calm. "No, no, not exactly. At this point, we would prefer not to have to do such a thing, but there is great risk if you do not learn to control your powers. Perhaps Fenris might take you to a certain place within the Other where you might develop that control?"

Fenris rumbled, "I know the place of which you speak, but if I take her there for training, how do I know that she'll be given the proper time and chances? What happens if this council decides too early that she is unfit to move on as a goddess?"

Thoth leaned forward, his broad hands folded under his chin. He exchanged glances with Thor, whose boisterous demeanor had changed to a frowning seriousness. The Egyptian answered for them all.

"If Bailey is unable to adequately master her powers and does not then agree to have them removed, she will be destroyed."

The girl opened her mouth to object, to tell them that she hadn't done anything wrong yet and she wanted to fulfill her role wisely and well. Fenris clamped a hand on her shoulder, pushed his way in front of her, and waved a hand dismissively.

"So be it." The wolf-father grunted. "I will take her to the training place. We go in peace."

After turning around, he took Bailey by the arm and led her out of the chamber. She started to pull away from him, so he hissed in her ear, "It's not worth arguing with them all. Not here, and not now. Let us make progress, and then we'll find them more amenable to hearing us out."

The girl was trembling with chaotic emotions. Nothing had gone the way she'd expected or hoped, but Fenris had never given her reason to mistrust him. She swallowed the outburst that had built up and followed him.

Once they were back out in the long blue hall, Fenris opened another portal. Bailey didn't know where it led, but she suspected it wasn't to Oregon.

"Come." The tall man waved her along and stepped into the glowing purple mass.

Blowing air out of her lungs, the girl did likewise. "Here goes nothing," she muttered.

CHAPTER TWO

The werewitch and the wolf-god emerged from the arcane doorway into what Bailey at first thought was Earth, but not the planet she was familiar with.

They were in a temperate green deciduous forest rather than the jungle of dead black jagged wood that covered most of the Other or the beautiful expanse of tall grass and ancient trees found on the holy land of the lycanthropic people. It wasn't even the hilly pine forest of her home. It looked like something out of a movie.

Overhead, the sky was about two-thirds covered by marbled clouds, but the rest was a normal blue. Beyond the tree line a short distance ahead, the girl glimpsed a vast open field of short, pale grass, in the center of which a massive castle loomed.

"The hell?" she wondered. "Did we go back in time? Is this somewhere in Europe?"

The overall feel of the place was medieval. The castle clearly came from that time period, with its broad stone walls seeming to enclose a town or marketplace, and another wall surrounding an inner bailey where the central keep loomed.

"No," Fenris said. "This is a divine training ground in a far, obscure corner of the Other." He gestured in turn at the woods, the plain, and the castle that was their likely destination. "It is a place without what you might call a true or essential form. Instead, it is conceptualized and manifested in accordance with the perspectives of those who occupy it."

She squinted. "*What?*" It wasn't that she had no idea what he meant; she got the gist. It just seemed like he ought to explain further.

He did. "Thanks to popular media and modern fiction, people from your civilization apparently think a magical training town ought to look like England in the High Middle Ages. Thus, it appears like that to you."

That had a certain logic to it. "Okay, fair enough. Training town, you said? I can already tell this is going to be different from when you taught me yourself in the swampy part of the Other."

The tall man strode forward, emerging from the trees onto the grassy sward with Bailey following close by his elbow. He enlarged on the situation as he walked.

"This is where beings who are empowered far beyond the norm for mortals come to learn and to refine and practice their skills. The goal is to permit them to be safe from inadvertently harming themselves or others during that time."

At last, Bailey felt that things *were* going the way she'd expected, as per what Fenris had told her before they'd gone to the gods' conclave. She just hoped that whatever awaited her would be less frustrating and confusing than their audience with the deific council had been.

A question popped into her brain.

"Wait," she queried, "why didn't I know about this place before? Why didn't you bring me here when we first started out, I mean?"

The tall man shook his head. "You did not qualify at the time. A werewitch is a rare thing, much more powerful than a human or even a regular were-shaman, but your potential still fell within the bounds of what was achievable for a being born of flesh. Now..." His voice trailed off.

For whatever reason, it sank in—the sheer scale and magnitude of what had happened. Bailey was at least as far above her past werewitch self as a werewitch was above a human. Perhaps farther. She'd avoided thinking about it until this moment.

I've known Fenris for a while, she mused, *and though I was aware of his godhood and all, he mostly seemed like a man. He restrains himself all the time. Being around him didn't prepare me for what godhood is, but I guess he's aiming to remedy that.*

Fenris went on, "It's a place for demigods, newborn gods and goddesses, and things that fall between the cracks. It provides for anything of deity-level power that needs to learn to channel its supreme might. Within, you will meet allies and begin a variety of courses, including staged battles somewhat like gladiatorial combat."

Part of her was thrilled by that, though she wasn't crazy enough to be fearless about it, either.

"It will be difficult, but if you succeed in taming the chaos that churns within you, you will be a full goddess in fact, whether recognized as such by certain other deific personalities or not. Oh, and succeeding does not necessarily entail triumphing in every combat. It is not a winner-takes-all elimination, but a process of growth in which there might be many winners."

She nodded, unable to think of anything to say to that.

"For now," Fenris concluded, "it will be enough to have control and internal stability. You will be more than capable of managing your responsibilities as High Shaman and ministering to both the Weres and the witches who have thrown in their lot with you."

The gate leading through the castle's outer wall was open, and the pair walked straight through into an area that reminded Bailey of the Oregon Renaissance Faire, though not as jolly.

They'd taken only half a dozen steps when two hulking creatures emerged from shadowed nooks to greet them. The humanoid figures of solid stone, eight or nine feet tall, were imposing, but their demeanor wasn't hostile.

"Stone golems," said Fenris, "who guard this place by acting as nullifiers of magic. They're tough to destroy with brute force, and spells don't work on them. To defeat one would require the true power and full creativity of a god. They act as both guards and wardens here, protecting the training grounds from external threats, and also keeping the trainees in. The beings who test themselves here aren't allowed to run off if the powers that be consider them a potential threat. Those who do try to desert end up having to deal with them."

As they passed the grim colossi, Bailey decided she'd keep that in mind. She didn't particularly want to "deal" with them, at least, not until she knew how.

Various figures bustled between the primitive buildings and the myriad tents. Most looked human, more or less; others were difficult to describe. They wore clothes and equipment representing all different cultures and time periods, including some the girl could not recognize.

Many were dressed for battle, decked out in armor of one kind or another and girded with a dizzying assortment of weapons. A few looked at her, nodded at her, or made brief comments that her mind failed to register as she trudged through the hubbub. The majority paid her no heed. They were busy with other things.

Bailey and Fenris moved toward the inner wall, attached to which was a stone building that she supposed was an exterior manor or guardhouse. A tall, blank-faced man in colorful clothes met them at the door and led them through a maze of dim halls. They ended at a wooden portal to a room.

"Madam," the host drawled, "please take your ease in here, and wait until you are called upon."

The chamber was better-appointed than she would have guessed, with a sumptuous bed, stacks of books, racks of clothing, and an assortment of pitchers and mirrors, like the room of a noble lady in a period drama.

She breathed out and sat on the bed. "So, I guess I wait. What about you?"

Fenris gazed at her, his shadowed face enigmatic and unresponsive. "I can stay here with you if you wish. I do not need to rest much, but a bedroll on the floor is enough for when I do. I can advise you to the best of my ability, and to the extent I'm allowed. I know how this place works."

"Okay, then." She shrugged. It occurred to her that this meant sleeping in the same room as a man who wasn't her boyfriend, but he wasn't really a *man*, after all. She'd never gotten any sense that he had the usual mortal urges.

The wolf-father allowed himself a bittersweet smile. "I came into existence *as* a god. I've never been anything else, so I was not subjected to testing here. Still, I can help you."

The girl laid her head on the pillow. "You always have, and you know I appreciate it."

He nodded. "Get some rest. Relax. It won't be long before they begin."

Agent Velasquez sat leaning back in his chair, his feet in their polished black shoes up and resting on the desk before his computer monitor. The goddamn machine was taking the usual length of time—namely, forever—to analyze a bunch of data and then spit out the appropriate reams of paperwork, all of which would need to be filled out by hand. He wasn't enthusiastic about it.

For the time being, though, there was nothing else to do.

Beside him sat another man, perhaps seven or eight years younger than Velasquez's thirty-six. Both were lean and athletic and an inch or two under six feet. Both had black hair, though Velasquez's was perilously close to "medium" length, the maximum allowable by the Agency.

The other man, of Korean descent, was lighter-complected, and his hair still bore a residual buzzcut from his recent military career. He had high sharp cheekbones, and his eyes were everywhere at once behind his standard-issue dark glasses.

It was good, Velasquez thought, that his new partner was the vigilant type, but he didn't need to be on the lookout at a time like this. Not when they were safe within the bowels of the Western division's headquarters beneath an unmarked building in Reno, Nevada.

"So," Agent Park began, "do you guys actually *do* anything here? *Is* there anything to do? It wasn't long ago I heard the organization was at war with some kind of terrorist group out of France. I'm not seeing a lot of action at the moment."

Velasquez grinned sardonically. "No, Park. There's nothing. It's very, very boring. You got in at exactly the right time, and for that, you ought to be grateful. Sit back and relax. You're getting paid. And compared to how things have been for too damn long lately, *peace* is a nice change of pace."

Park scowled. "I'm glad America is safe if that's what you mean, but I didn't join the Agency for the purpose of sitting around collecting a paycheck while barely doing any work. Can't we, I dunno, do a patrol or a scouting mission?"

"Later," Velasquez remarked. "Technology does a lot of the legwork for us in that regard. As I understand it, that's increasingly how things are in the military too, isn't it?"

Park scratched the back of his neck. "Pretty much."

"Anyway," the older agent went on, "let me tell you a story. Well, to be fair, there's, like, a whole set of stories about a certain natural disaster we call 'Hurricane Bailey.' Our predecessors in this office, Agents Townsend and

Spall, dealt with her for months before I stepped into Townsend's shoes and she fell straight into my lap."

Park squinted in mock confusion. "So, you're saying you have a problem with a hot twenty-something brunette falling into your lap?"

"In this particular case," Velasquez shot back, "*yes*. Good Lord, yes. You can't deal with her and *not* have a problem because she is, like, a walking catalog of problems. A shit-storm in humanoid form."

The younger agent asked, "Then why not take her out?"

Velasquez shook his head. "It isn't like that. She's...a pretty good person, truth be told. The crap she caused wasn't intentional. It's more like her mere existence attracts all kinds of assholes and causes everything to get fucked up beyond all recognition. FUBAR, right?"

Park grunted.

"Thus," the other continued, "since we can't justify taking her out, we have no choice but to let her traipse around, exercising her natural talent for, and I guess inalienable right to, attract a metric shit-ton of fuckassery. In a way, she was indirectly responsible for one of our predecessors getting killed—Spall. Lots of other guys, too. Not that I blame her, since we worked with her against the Venatori in the end. Let's just say it might have been better if she'd stayed a random hick werewolf girl in the mountains instead of becoming the paranormal equivalent of Kanye or whichever other dumbass celebrity is currently making the whole country catch a cold every time they sneeze. Why? Because if she's involved with something, that means we get to deal with a situation where agents might potentially die. Do you want to die, Park?"

"Not particularly," the younger man admitted. "I'm not afraid to lay down my life if I have to, but surviving is better than not surviving, yeah."

Velasquez looked at him and nodded slowly. "Good. You're a smart man. Since we have all this free time, we can spend it getting damn good at an important skill every agent worth his salt should develop."

Park looked itchy at the prospect of having activities to focus on. "And what's that?"

The older man grinned and held up his mobile device. "*Pong.* Check it out. One of the boys in Tech dug this out of whatever Mayan-era crypt it was buried in. I'll send it to your phone. The brilliant, elegant simplicity of it almost brings a tear to my eye."

Park finally laughed, and five minutes later, the two men were engrossed in a desperate struggle of electronic table tennis.

"Yes!" the younger agent cheered. "That's four out of six for me so far. Are we betting on this?"

"Are you kidding, Park?" asked Velasquez. "Gambling is against the law. Devoted public servants such as us would never lower ourselves to—wait, how much you willing to lose?"

They haggled over terms and eventually decided on a pot of two dollars.

After the games resumed, with Velasquez bringing the roster back to a tie, he muttered more to himself than his new partner, "It has probably been *too* quiet lately. Makes me wonder if we only got through the first half of Hurricane Bailey and we're currently in the eye of the storm."

Park won the next round. "I'm about to be two dollars

richer," he gloated. "Wait, one dollar. You know what I mean."

"We'll see about that." Velasquez returned to the competition at hand, but a notion entered his head that maybe the entire first hurricane was over...and a second, much bigger one was on the way. After all, the girl had technically attained godhood at the end of their last encounter. The next shitstorm might be the Apocalypse.

He pursed his lips as Park defeated him again. "I wonder," he contemplated, "If I should binge-watch Netflix on my next day off and finish a bunch of shit on my queue while there still *is* a Netflix to watch."

Who knew what tomorrow would bring?

"What in the names of all the powers of the multiverse," Thor wondered, "are we going to do about her? I *like* her, but I understand the risks. And there are reasons Fenris does not sit on this council. We mustn't forget that he is the one who's mentored her."

Loki stared at the war-god with heavily lidded eyes and a mouth twisted in sardonic exasperation. "Could be worse," he remarked. "At least she hasn't tried to solve every problem by hitting it with a hammer."

"Be silent, Loki," Freya snapped. The red-bearded giant bristled with antagonism on Loki's behalf. "We all understand what Thor speaks of. Now, does anyone have anything *useful* to add to the discussion?"

Coyote made a low sound in his throat and tilted his head to the side before he spoke, his twinkling eyes distant.

"I do not think there *is* a safe option, but when is anything guaranteed to be entirely safe? If we look only at her raw power, she is not much of a threat to all of us together. Aradia was a lesser deity, and the girl failed to absorb *all* of her essence, just most of it. If we examine Bailey's attitude and her actions, she just seems like a pleasant, even rather innocent young woman."

Balder, who claimed innocence as part of his symbolic portfolio, raised a finger. "A pleasant young woman who took many lives while waging a war, and killed a divinity, too. Justified it might have been, but she is far from harmless."

"Yes," Coyote agreed. "There is about her an aura of disturbance, wrongness, and chaos. It may not be attached to her, but it follows her. It is as though a tear in the fabric of the cosmic order found its way to her little valley, and she leaped into it and travels by way of its movements. I wish no ill to her, but I grow weary of the types of strife she seems to precipitate again and again. Were I able, I would mend the wound in the cosmos around her and leave the girl alone."

Thor grunted and fluffed his beard. "I do not like this discussion," he announced; as always, he spoke louder than any other deity present, his volume much greater than necessary. "Makes me feel odd and unmanned. Deciding someone's fate when they aren't here to give an account of themselves. Cowardly, I say. It reeks of dung and drips with slime."

Balder and Freya exchanged glances. The Lady of Sorcery spoke.

"Bailey has been unpredictable, and that alone is

hazardous for one of her power." The green in her eyes sharpened. "And Thor is right about one thing. She has been instructed by—forgive me, Loki—the one who is prophesied to bring about Ragnarök. True, Fenris had done nothing overt to expedite the disaster, nor given any indication that he desires it to happen, but it *is* part of his mantle. Wherever he goes and whatever he is invested in, our eyes should follow him and watch for anything untoward. We cannot afford the luxury of trust."

For the moment, the eyes of the other deities went to the one who had fathered the wolf-god.

Loki rolled his eyes and steepled his long fingers. "This again. Haven't we been over it? The pup is no concern of ours," he snickered at the pun, "and *especially* not of mine. What he's up to is none of our business beyond immediate threats. If Bailey perpetrates some mid-level mischief on the mortal plane, what of it? Why should we care? So be it, I say."

The trickster god stood up from his chair and made ready to leave. When he was halfway across the white chamber, he turned back and looked at the other five.

"Besides," he appended, "a little more mischief is worth the trouble. Think about how boring things would become without it. We'll have a laugh! Far too few of those lately."

With that, Loki departed, and the remaining gods waited in silence until he had left the room.

Thoth rubbed one broad hand over the other, and the muscles along his square jaw rippled. "We do not need to take drastic action yet," he intoned, "but the girl should be watched by pupils of ours or people representing our respective pantheons, trusted servants and emissaries and peacekeepers."

"Yes," agreed Balder, "that is wise. I know of a certain hero who can go incognito on my behalf into the training town and pose as a fellow inductee. He shall have no orders but to observe."

Thoth nodded. "I will do the same. And if Bailey is a threat, there might be a way to mitigate the potential damage without causing her unnecessary harm."

Coyote raised a bushy eyebrow. "Oh? How?"

CHAPTER THREE

The Camaro's engine purred as the driver shifted into park, then fell silent. The door opened and out stepped Gunney, proprietor of Gunney's Auto Shop, who stood for a moment admiring the way the vehicle looked on the dusty back lot of his business.

"It's a beauty, isn't it? I almost thought she'd go for red, but hard to go wrong with basic black."

Roland, who'd just parked his Audi, shrugged. "I would have gone with green. Or white, of course. I might still get the Audi repainted."

"Meh," said the short, aging mechanic. He scratched his beard and took off his grimy old baseball cap, allowing the breeze to cool his shaggy head before pulling it back on. "Color's less important than how it drives, and it handles better than it looks. I would know since Bailey and I practically rebuilt the thing from scratch."

The wizard rubbed his nose. "I suppose someone has to work on cars. Machines aren't my thing. They're like a different kind of magic that I never bothered to study.

Anyway, thanks for coming to the car's rescue. You know how Fenris is. The problems of mere mortals aren't of much concern when he feels he needs to drag one of them off into a parallel dimension."

Gunney snorted, shaking his head, and led Roland into the shop office, where the two of them raided the fridge for sodas. They both left the orange pop in glass bottles alone; that was Bailey's favorite. Roland preferred lemon-lime, and Gunney was a cola man.

"I wonder," Roland mused as he sipped, relishing the cool evening breeze that had begun to dispel the day's heat, "what the hell she's getting up to? I don't like leaving her alone, though I'm not sure two gods need my help."

The older man raised his eyebrows. "Probably not. I still can hardly believe it. It's strange; I've lived in this town for years, and right from the start, I somehow knew things here were *different*. A detail here, a glimpse of an oddity there, and one day I came to realize that I believed in frickin' werewolves and didn't mind having them as neighbors.

"But these last few months? Shit on a shingle. Witch wars and alternate universes and gods dying and being born. We've gone beyond the *Twilight Zone* all the way to the funny farm."

The wizard stretched his long legs. "Something like that, yeah."

"Anyhow," Gunney went on, "want to take your mind off all this crap by tinkering with a few cars? Might be educational."

Roland laughed. "Uh, thanks, but I'd advise against that.

With my skill or lack thereof, your shop would become less of a car hospital and more of a car torture chamber."

The mechanic let out a short bark of laughter. "Fair enough. What'll you do instead?"

Both men knew that he meant, what would he do to help Bailey in her absence?

The wizard dropped his empty soda bottle into the recycle bin.

"Admittedly, I'm unsure at this point. In the past, I had an inkling of an idea, a starting point from which to proceed. At present, I'm fumbling around in the dark. Fenris popped in and said some vague portentous doomy shit, then both of them hopped through a portal and were gone. I don't know where they went or if she needs anything. With things having been so peaceful, I was hoping she and I could spend more time together, so I'm bitter and curmudgeonly about the whole thing."

Gunney thought it over for a couple of seconds. "You could go tell her brothers what happened. They deserve to know. That'd be a good start."

"Yes," Roland acceded, "I'll do that, for starters. And maybe, say, reach out to our friends around the region, since we haven't seen half of them since the conclusion of the whole Aradia affair. It wouldn't hurt to have them thinking kindly of us in case we need them to leap to our aid."

The mechanic shot him a meaningful look. "That's borderline Machiavellian, but it's a good idea. You've helped them, and they've helped you. Get to it, city boy. I'll hold the fort."

Roland waved and headed back to his new car,

reflecting that Gunney's shop had been used as a fort during two different attacks by the Venatori. The damage from those ugly incidents had been repaired, and no real signs remained of the sleepy town's brief status as a war zone.

He drove the few minutes to the far northwest corner of Greenhearth, where the Nordin family house awaited. Their pole barn had become his permanent guest room, and though he had no plans to leave Bailey, he wondered if he ought to get a proper job and acquire his own place.

Or perhaps he and Bailey could get a place together.

It was an old farmhouse in decent condition at the edge of a residential neighborhood, and the grass at the rear of the lot rose with the foothills to blend with the wooded mountains beyond. Jacob, the eldest of Bailey's three younger brothers, held the front door open as he approached.

"Hi," Jacob greeted him. "Where's Bailey?"

"Oh, the usual," said Roland. "A big guy stepped out of a purple hole in the sky and made her come with him to talk to some gods or something. You know how it goes."

The young werewolf did not fail to believe him, and once the wizard was inside, he related the whole story to the three of them. Besides Jacob, Russell and Kurt, the middle and youngest brothers, respectively, were home. All were tall and craggy and stubbly, though Russell was tallest and darkest of the three and Kurt the thinnest.

Russell grunted. "Sounds bad."

"Well," Roland elaborated, "Fenris said that the other deities were in the middle of their little teachers' conference already, so he didn't want to waste time. Bailey said she'd send word if she needed help. Not sure how."

"Usually," Kurt snarked in his usual smartass fashion, "it's other people who need help because of her. If we're really worried, we can always pray to her."

Jacob threw a beer can at his younger brother's head.

"Ow," said Kurt.

The eldest turned to Roland. "I'm worried too, but there's not much we can do. She's capable of taking care of herself, and Fenris usually knows what's best. Let's wait and see how things look by tomorrow. You crashing here tonight?"

"Uh, maybe," Roland waffled. "I want to talk to some of our pals in Seattle first and check in with them. Then I'll decide."

Jacob shrugged, and the wizard bid the three farewell.

"Careful," Russell growled. He meant well; growling was his normal way of speaking.

For no particular reason, Roland got back into his car and drove out to an isolated spot in the woods a quarter-mile off the main highway. It wasn't far from where he and Bailey had been jumped by about twenty asshole Weres in league with the crime ring they'd antagonized months ago. The pricks had messed his face up, but his magic, combined with the wonders of modern medicine, had undone the damage quite nicely.

The wizard sat in the growing shadows, then pulled out his phone and dialed Dante Viari, a fellow caster he'd met up in Rain City five or six weeks ago in the runup to the fight with Aradia. They'd kept in touch extensively at first, but it had been a good two weeks since their last conversation.

Dante picked up. "Hello. Roland?"

"Yeah, it's me. I wanted to, like, check in on how things are going with the whole witch community in the Pacific Northwest and if things are still cool with our furry friends. Anything interesting come over the grapevine? You're the man to ask."

The other wizard audibly inhaled through his nose. "Umm, no, things are okay for the most part. I did hear about some witches who went missing in Portland, but that's a bit of a drive from Seattle, and I just got it from the local gossip today. I haven't checked it out yet."

Roland frowned in the gathering darkness.

"But," Dante's voice went on, "definitely no more fuck-heads targeting Weres, so all quiet on that front. People are getting along fine; the worst of the tension is gone. No reason to suspect it'll change."

The older caster sighed, unbuckled his seatbelt, and stepped out of the car, pacing along the damp earth as he talked. "Okay, good. Regarding the missing witches, were you *planning* on looking into it?"

"Yep," replied Dante. "Why, you and Bailey wanna help?"

"Bailey's busy, but I'd be happy to get out of town for a while." He smiled, thinking that it would also be an opportunity to rebuild goodwill with the sorcerous community. He'd practically gone native among Weres since he met Bailey. "In fact, if you're up to meeting me in Portland tonight, we can do that, or tomorrow's fine."

Dante considered. "Tomorrow. I'll try to get up early.

It's about three times farther to Portland for me than for you. I'll text you when I'm on my way."

"Sounds good. Bye." Roland hung up. It was true, the Rose City was only about an hour and twenty minutes from Greenhearth.

As such, he figured he'd get the drive out of the way tonight. Heading over there on a nice peaceful evening reminded him of the day he and Bailey had met. He decided he'd even spend the night in the motel they'd rented.

"Christ," he mumbled under his breath as he started up the engine, "she's only been gone for, like, six hours, not six weeks. Get hold of yourself, man."

―――――

Bailey's eyes fluttered open. The bed in her room in the stone manor was probably the most comfortable she'd ever slept on. She yawned, stretched, and sat up.

Fenris was seated at the small wooden table within the room, a steaming pot of tea and two cups before him. "I thought you'd rise soon," he commented.

The girl rubbed her eyes and trudged over to the table. "Thanks. I'm more of a coffee girl, but tea gets the job done okay. And you make it well."

He poured her a cup. She'd drunk about half of it when there were knocks on several doors throughout the hallway, including hers.

A valet shouted, presumably speaking to multiple rooms, "All trainees and new wards of the castle are to assemble for orientation at once."

Bailey walked to the door and opened it. The same man who'd escorted her yesterday was standing in the corridor, watching other people shuffle out of their rooms. He glared at Bailey, who hesitated.

The girl looked at Fenris, arching an eyebrow.

"Go," said the wolf-god. "I am famished, and you know the food of civilized people isn't to my taste. I'll hunt in the woods for my breakfast. It's guaranteed fresh that way." He smiled with his teeth, showing off his inner wolf.

The girl mimicked the expression. "Shit, I kinda want to join you. It's been forever since I hunted for food."

The blank-faced valet cleared his throat. "No, young lady, you will not join him. You are to report immediately. You'll be allowed to eat later if circumstances permit. Come!"

Taken aback, she almost cussed the man out but forced herself to bite down on such a stupid reaction. The powers that ran the place must have good reasons for running it the way they did.

"Okay, fine," she muttered.

Bailey followed the attendant and the rest of the crowd through the hall and out into the broad yard before the manor. She examined her co-trainees. They were a strange and diverse crew, though all fairly young, in their twenties or thirties. They'd formed a line. Bailey stood near the far end on the right.

The quality of light suggested mid-morning, though despite the half-clear sky, there was no sun that Bailey could see. She supposed an enchanted realm didn't need one, based on Old England though it was.

A man stamped up before them, dressed in full steel

plate armor, hefting a large black mace in one hand and a large white shield in the other. Most of his face was hidden by his helmet, but a butt-chin and scowling mouth were visible.

"Some of you," he announced in a loud, imperious voice, "have met me before. For those who are meeting me for the first time, know that I am your trainer. My name is Malkeg Ironfist, and my job is to whip you upstarts, with your power incontinence and your beginner's luck and your general ignorance, into proper shape. Proud as you might be of your cosmically empowered asses, they are still the pink behinds of amateurs as far as the heavyweight players are concerned."

Oh, fuck, Bailey thought. *The gods studied the Marine Corps and took notes on how to train people. This is gonna be tons of fun.*

"Some of you," Malkeg said again, "are demigods, or fledgling gods-to-be, or mighty half-breeds, or who knows whatever the fuck else. I do not care. I will teach you to control your powers. I will *make* you control your powers, because if your sorry asses cannot, consider that asses can explode. Then there's projectile shit flying everywhere, and no one needs or wants that, particularly with the amount of arcane strength you children are capable of putting behind your supernatural diarrhea."

A couple of guys snickered, and Malkeg glared at them until they shut up. Then he continued his spiel.

"I'm going to run you ragged," he vowed. "In combat, in labor, in mental exercises; intensive training of all sorts. Make damn sure you listen because if you can do that one simple thing, then you *might* qualify for godhood, complete with realms and mantles and portfolios. It's a possibility for some of you, namely, those who can put duty before themselves. An understanding of duty is a thing you'll need."

Bailey felt borderline relieved. As a shaman, duty was paramount. She had a head start.

Malkeg waved his mace in the air. "Now, *run!* Move! You'll get breakfast after. Go, you cretins! *Run, fucks!*"

The trainees who'd been here a while fell smoothly into a fast jog. The newbies all started, then broke into a sprint to catch up with their fellows. The line of initiates moved across the castle's outer grounds, through the gates (and under the watchful eyes of the anti-magic golems), and out onto the moorland beyond.

Their trainer jogged along behind them, keeping pace despite his heavy armor. "To the woods! Straight through the middle. And pay attention to what you're doing!"

The column ran into the center of the forest. Bailey, near the back of the formation, heard a couple guys up front issuing a warning to the people near them, but they used a language unknown to her.

The light dimmed as they entered the thick forest with its old dark-green hardwood trees. There were no sounds of birds or insects, only the stamping of feet and the huffing of breath. Nothing happened 'til they'd gone deep enough into the woods for the sward and the castle to fall out of sight.

Then the shadows came alive and attacked.

"Shit!" Bailey gasped. She'd been growing a little short on breath, cursing herself for having relied too much on magic and not enough on physical activity recently, and the ambush caught her by surprise. Screams and curses went around the group.

Wraiths, the indigenous pests of the Other.

The werewitch had fought small armies of them alongside Roland, but she was rusty, and these somehow seemed larger, nastier, and more frightening. The inky black of their semi-liquid forms suggested horribly deformed faces, gaping mouths, and reaching claws.

The godlings had no weapons, so in their panic, they retaliated with huge blasts of magic. Raw elemental force engulfed half the forest, blasting the wraiths into oblivion. Explosions chained together until mushroom clouds rose into the sky. Tornadoes sucked up mountains of debris. The sky turned white with lightning.

Bailey turned to a trio of wraiths near her and swept out her hand, intending to hit them with a modest wave of concussive force combined with flame since the creatures seemed vulnerable to heat and light.

Instead, a nuclear holocaust erupted before her, blasting four dozen trees into whitening cinders riding a rippling shockwave. The wraiths had simply vanished. The earth had turned black. Deafening and blinding, the destruction and chaos she'd unleashed scared her more than the attack had.

Then it was over, and the trainees stood looking upon a bare and ravaged wasteland and gibbering at each other.

The trees grew back in the space of what seemed like minutes, as though they were watching a time-lapse spread out over a hundred years.

Malkeg barked, "Move on! Did I tell you to stop and gawk?"

They obeyed.

The forest's shadows attacked them three more times, and in each case, they reacted by destroying everything around them. Bailey tried to restrain herself better, but it appeared that her magic had four or five times the power for half the effort now.

Nonetheless, after what felt like hours of running, fighting, and occasionally leaping over ravines or piles of rock, everyone was exhausted when they emerged from the woods. As they stumbled back toward the castle, the forest rose behind them, betraying no sign of the terrible wrath to which it had been subjected.

Malkeg finally called a halt once they were within the castle's outer wall and a stone's throw beyond the golems. The trainees struggled not to collapse.

"You fucking idiots!" Malkeg roared. "Piss-poor performance, all of you. Oh, sure, you're great and mighty gods and goddesses or whatever, and you have the power to blow away anything that jumps out at you. Is that what you're going to do when your followers beg you for help? Nuke their city in the process of saving it?"

Bailey frowned, but she got the point.

"You'll have to try again," Ironfist went on, "but next time, you need to *focus* your strength and either take out specific targets or work in subtler ways. You can't just be walking bombs set to explode at any moment. For now, go eat."

The crowd started to disperse. In the past, Bailey had noticed that the Other suppressed the needs of the body, but this place was different; she was starving.

"Yes, sir," she murmured, then followed the others toward the mess hall.

The werewitch sat down at the end of a long wooden table within a crude but oddly cozy structure that was half-building, half-tent, a wooden framework with cloth in place of walls. In front of her was a broad platter heaped with food and an equally large flagon of sparkling cider. The entities who managed the castle didn't skimp on rations. She'd assembled an impressive deli tray of meats, cheeses, pieces of hard bread-like crackers, as well as sliced fruits, berries, and a cup of yogurt. She tore into the feast as soon as her ass touched the bench.

Midway into her repast, a man came up beside her. She glanced his way, seeing a tall, muscular young man with ebony skin, a shaved head, and, she realized with curiosity, heterochromia. His left eye was a very dark brown, while his right eye was a light hazel-orange.

"May I sit down?" he asked. His voice was higher than she'd expected, smooth and pleasant. She nodded and he sat next to her, leaving about a foot and a half between them.

She extended a hand and swallowed the food in her mouth. "I'm Bailey Nordin. I'm new."

He took her hand in a firm grasp. "Carl Robertson, a scion. And what's your story?"

She cocked an eyebrow, confused. "What do you mean by that, exactly? Your question, that is, plus I dunno what a 'scion' is."

"I was asking what you were," he explained. "As for what I am, I'm the product of one supernatural being mating with another. 'Scion' is the common term. In my case, my father was a shapeshifter who seduced a minor witch goddess. That makes me like a demigod, only minus any human element."

"Huh," Bailey marveled. "Never heard of you guys." She also felt a pang of dread at the mention of witch-goddesses. How many of them were there? If Freya and Aradia weren't the only ones, the Venatori might find a new patron.

Carl smiled. "Most people haven't, but that's fine. So, yeah. I'm part paranormal monster, part deity, which conveniently gives me immense magical potential, combined with all the usual shapeshifter powers: extra strength, and of course, the ability to change form."

"Nice," Bailey commented. If he was telling the truth, she felt less impressive next to him, but also less unusual and lonely. "Shapeshifter, as in, you have an animal form? Or, like, you can mimic anyone, like a doppelganger?"

"More the latter," he responded. "My powers have grown lately. I could already control the shifting ones well enough, but now my witch side is getting stronger, which is why I'm here. Honestly, I don't know how to control both types of magic yet."

The girl shook her head. "I thought I'd seen and heard everything. That's interesting, Carl, and I'm being honest. As for why I asked about the shifter thing, it's because I'm a werewolf. Well, werewitch. And shaman. I killed a goddess and absorbed most of her powers."

Carl blinked in mild surprise. He listened, relaxed but

curious, as she related the gist of her background and what had led up to her presence here. She decided that she liked him. With guys like Malkeg in charge and some of the other students conversing in foreign tongues, it would help to have a nice person around who spoke English to boot.

"So," Bailey concluded, "I think I can handle whatever they have in store, but I have to wonder what's next."

"Same," said Carl.

They got their answer a moment later. One of the brightly-dressed valets came in and shouted at them to assemble outside the castle's inner gates. It was time for their next training session.

Bailey grimaced. "Damn. I was hoping we'd have time to digest the food as well as eat it."

Carl sighed. "Oh, joy."

CHAPTER FOUR

Bailey, Carl, and the others lined up in the yard before the manor once again. This time, rows of mannequins had been set up and appointed with all manner of clothing, armor, and utility gear. Beside and behind the dummies were racks of weapons.

Out came Malkeg Ironfist, still clad head to toe in steel.

"All right, O mighty divine ones," he growled, with exaggerated sarcasm, "it's time to suit up as you see fit. Take your pick from the selection we have here. You're about to be thrown into combat in a place where all our magic—yes, including mine—will react in *interesting* ways."

Bailey assumed that when Malkeg said "interesting," what he meant was "bad."

"Choose wisely," the trainer continued. "Not that I'm going to *help* you choose. Some of this armor can shed magic like water off a duck's back, meaning you'd have to use a lot more arcane energy to see the same effects or smaller effects. Among these weapons, we have ones that can bat spells aside, resist enchantments, or cut through arcane fields. The section of the Other we're headed to warps magic oddly for gods as well as mortals. Deities occasionally go there to settle their differences on a more level playing field, because everything is fucked up there."

Carl smiled. "Sounds like a *great* place," he whispered.

Malkeg marched back and forth. "Therefore," he concluded, "this exercise will allow you all to train without resorting to total planetary annihilation every time a bird shits on your head. It'll also teach you to be creative and fight in other ways, not rely on overpowered magic all the fucking time. That's folly—a common one, as it happens, among gods who were born into godhood. I expect better of your kind."

Bailey thought back to Aradia. The Venatori Order's deity had arrogantly relied upon nothing but spellcraft and the fanatical loyalty of her followers, and it had cost her everything once Bailey bled her dry of her arcane essence.

The werewitch went to suit up, deciding that Malkeg's program made a certain amount of sense.

She found some light armor that looked like leather that fit relatively snugly over her normal clothes but was constructed in a way that offered good mobility. To give herself more protection, she added a cloak whose outer side was covered with interlocking metal scales that shimmered with a brightness beyond anything normal.

"Hey," she called to the trainer, "what does this thing do? What are these scale things?"

Ironfist looked at her with vague, patronizing contempt, as if he'd expected her to keep her mouth shut and play Russian Roulette with her selections, but he answered the question.

"The scales," he elucidated, "like most pieces of metal, are hard to cut or pierce. They also will deflect certain types of magical attacks, mostly things like heat, cold, electricity, and arcanoplasm. Doesn't deflect *physics*, though. An explosion might not burn you, but it'd still throw you far enough to bust open your head."

She nodded. "Okay. Thanks."

For her weapons, she chose a pair of double-edged short swords. She didn't know much about pre-modern weaponry, but she guessed they were from the Viking Age or thereabouts. They weren't too heavy, but with her extra Were strength, she was able to flick them around like knives. She wasn't used to dual wielding, but two weapons meant she'd still have one if she lost the other.

Finally, she found a round steel shield a foot or so in diameter and strapped it on her left wrist and forearm. If offered protection without taking up a hand or hampering her movements.

She glanced up and saw Carl. He'd donned a tunic of brigandine, dotted with studs that held thin metal strips within the fabric and reinforced vulnerable areas on his limbs and torso with partial steel plate. He also wore a helmet with an open front and carried a heavy mace, much like Malkeg's. Oddly, he had neither a shield nor a second weapon, but then Bailey saw a big, scary, spiked gauntlet on his left hand. It was a weapon in itself, and it would allow him to grab other people's incoming armaments.

Malkeg looked around. "Everyone ready? If not, hurry the hell up! Find someone else to fasten your armor if you can't do it yourself. We leave at two hundred."

He began loudly counting upwards from "one,"

stomping back and forth in front of the trainees to rush them along. Bailey and Carl checked each other's armor and found it to be fitted properly, though neither of them was expert. They'd have to hope for the best.

Everyone stood at attention when Malkeg was only at "ninety-seven," so he stopped counting and ordered them to follow him through the inner gates to a domed structure near the keep. Within was a wide and glowing portal of deep violet light. "In," the trainer barked.

Bailey and Carl were among the first to hold their breath and step through.

For whatever reason, Bailey had expected to find herself in a hellish waste of eldritch weirdness, but in fact, it was more like an illustration from a book of fairytales. It was an English forest, dense but not gloomy, lush, lovely, and full of wildlife noises, though no beasts or birds or bees were in sight. The sun shone overhead. The air was on the cusp between warm and cool.

Good fighting weather, the girl decided.

Then she realized that she was alone. The portal had sent the trainees to different locations at random.

Malkeg materialized right behind her and she jumped, startled.

"You've all been displaced," he barked, and she wondered if this were him, or an astral holograph; it was hard to be sure. "This event is a *battle royale* for supremacy among you. Killing is not permitted; you may only batter your opponents into submission or unconsciousness.

Those who yield or surrender are to be spared further violence. Beyond that, there are no rules. Fight, and survive."

The werewitch's palms sweated within her leather gloves, and she twirled her swords to get a better feel for them.

Malkeg's image went on, "Winners and losers will be decided by us."

"How?" Bailey asked.

The big knight glared at her as he flickered. It was a projection after all, but she'd drawn the real Malkeg's attention. "Don't ask me that, girl." The image flickered again, and she was once more looking at a message broadcast to every participant.

"Other trainers as well as I will be watching you, scoring points and keeping track of your endeavors. Watch your asses. Be ready. Go!"

Malkeg vanished and a horn blew, its note in a disturbing warble. The games began.

Bailey walked forward. One direction seemed as good as any other until she met her first opponent.

A long skirmish of ambushes and one-on-one duels, she surmised. *Hoo, boy.*

She met her first adversary all of fifteen steps from her starting point. Or, rather, she heard them.

Whoever they were, they must have over-armored themself, since the clanking, jangling, and scraping was obvious well before she saw the individual. Bailey drew in her breath and fell behind a thick tree trunk opposite the direction from which the racket came. She peered around the edge.

A stout individual, most likely a man and about her height of five foot eight, was tanking his way forward, making no effort at stealth. He wore full plate armor, probably over mail, and a great helm that hid his face. Additionally, he carried a big kite shield and an arming sword with a finely-tapered point capable of piercing all but the thickest and strongest armor.

Bailey would have to be careful. There was no way her swords could cut through so much steel.

Not that I'm supposed to kill the bastard anyway. Clonking him in the head and pinning him to the ground ought to be good enough. She nodded to herself.

The helmet limited the man's vision. The werewitch hung back, creeping around the tree as he approached so the wooden trunk remained between her and him. He gave no sign of having seen her.

Once he was two or three steps beyond her, she leaped out, arms wheeling as she swung her swords toward the back of his helmet. He started to turn around, and the blades caught him in the side of the head as his shield pushed out and threw her off-balance.

Both combatants reeled back. The armored man shook his head, the clang of steel on steel still ringing in the air. Bailey stumbled but found her feet again quickly enough. Then her foe tried to use magic.

He waved his sword and the air rippled. What should have been a half-fiery concussive burst came out as a weird snaking line of distortion. Still, it moved fast, and Bailey spun and raised her cloak to deflect it. The metal scales shone as they absorbed the brunt of the magic, and the physical impact of the projectile whipped the cloak back.

By then, Bailey was moving to avoid being struck. She jumped and kicked, her sword-arms coming down to prevent the man's sword and shield from rising toward her, and her booted foot struck him in the chest. He let out a loud *oof* and crashed into the tree, then slumped to the ground.

Bailey sprang atop him and leveled the point of a blade in front of his helmet's visor-slit. "Yield!" she snapped.

He groaned. "I yield."

She nodded and stepped back. "Smart man. Better luck next time, I guess." Then she moved on into the forest, seeking her next engagement.

Nine more trainees confronted her, and she overcame them all. Most of them had little if any experience at hand-to-hand combat, so they tended to panic and blunder into stupid mistakes or overexert themselves too quickly. The ones who tried to fight with magic found their spells badly weakened and hard to control. Once Bailey had to leap aside when an oak nearly fell on top of her. Someone's plasma lance had spun off-course and destroyed the trunk of the tree behind her.

She faced people as lightly armored as herself and as heavily armored as the first man, and people wielding light weapons or huge ones, everything from daggers and hand axes to scimitars, maces, spears, and swords. Two of the combatants she defeated were women. She couldn't say which were demigods, scions, and or other things she didn't know about yet.

She also suspected that her swords hit harder than they should have by rights. They might carry a slight enchantment that stacked arcane mass behind their blows.

The ninth man wore partial plate over mail and leather and a sallet helm and carried a two-handed greatsword of the late-medieval variety that was over five feet long, with a complex ringed hilt and parrying hooks past the blade's ricasso. He seemed athletic and understood the basic movements and positioning of a fight.

But he clearly had no experience using his huge weapon, and especially not in a dense forest. Confronting him, Bailey avoided being hit by the long blade by a couple hairs' breadth, and her eyes bulged as it whizzed beside her head. She jumped aside, realizing that if the man *did* strike her, with all his size and weight behind such a large sword, she was done for.

He didn't. She was able to whack him on the knee and in the armpit with a quick run-by attack, evading his slow counter. When he tried wheeling the sword around to use its momentum to strike faster, the tip glanced off a tree branch and screwed up his balance.

Bailey moved in, drove her armored knee into his codpiece, whacked him atop the helmet, and threw him face-first into a huge protruding root. He groaned in pain and dropped his sword, then slumped, unconscious.

"Good," she breathed. She couldn't recall how many people were participating in the melee, but having defeated nine of them, she had to be one of the frontrunners in the scoring process.

A short jog led her to sounds of combat; another pair of trainees was brawling ahead. The girl pushed through a screen of foliage and took in the scene at a glance.

It was Carl, locked in battle with someone of comparable size wearing heavy black lamellar armor and a helmet that looked vaguely Asian; she couldn't place it otherwise. The other guy carried a two-handed pole-hammer with a relatively large head and a nasty spike atop the shaft.

The black-armored guy clashed his longer weapon against Carl's one-handed mace, and before Carl could retaliate by grabbing the hammer with his gauntlet, the sheer force of the blow drove him to his knees. Then the guy in black kicked him from the side, bowling him over. He raised his hammer.

"Shit," Bailey gasped. Acting on instinct, she rushed forward to rescue her new friend, her body low to the ground but her swords held high.

Her intrusion distracted the knight. He started to pull back his overhead swing, and Carl seized the opportunity to raise his mace and knock the hammer aside.

Then Bailey piled into the other man, swept her cloak in front of his face to further disorient him, then kneed, kicked, and backhanded him in the head with her buckler. Meanwhile, Carl stuck the shaft of his mace between the man's ankles, and he toppled, cursing, to the ground.

"I yield," he grunted.

Bailey and Carl stood up and looked at each other.

"Y'know," the werewitch remarked, "I don't recall old Malkeg saying there was any rule against teaming up."

The scion grinned. "Me neither. Let's get 'em. You're faster, but I've got the thicker armor and a beefier weapon, so we'll say you go in first to throw them off, then I finish them."

"Sounds like a plan." She set off in the same direction she'd been going, and Carl followed close on her heels.

Soon they encountered one guy wearing a heavy helm but only a brigandine tunic, bracers, and shin guards. He wielded a hand-axe in his right hand and a dagger in his left. Bailey darted in to sweep the axe aside with her swords while Carl struck him in the center of the torso with his mace slightly outside the reach of the dagger, and the man fell to the ground, bruised and nauseated.

Carl accepted the fellow's surrender, and the pair set off.

Things rapidly grew more complicated, however. Other trainees had reached the same conclusion as Bailey and Carl and began working in small groups. No more lone fighters remained. The melee had become a team sport, a miniature clan war in which clusters of two to six clashed with one another.

Being only a pair, Bailey and Carl hung back from skirmishes with the larger groups, instead leading them into battle against other factions. Often, poorly-controlled magic flew when groups ran into each other, then the two of them moved in to finish off whoever remained.

As the bodies dropped and the surrenders flowed in, it seemed a long time passed without the werewitch and the scion encountering anyone. They surmised there must only be a handful of combatants still in the match. There had to be someone, or the trainers would have ended the bout.

They burst into a clearing and met their final opponents.

There were four of them in a line, three males and one female, all middlingly armored, much like Carl. The woman held a spear, two of the men gripped hand-and-a-half swords, and the fourth man hoisted a two-handed military flail.

"Hi," one of the swordsmen called. "Looks like we're the last ones. Now, we believe in a fair fight, so let's not use any magic that might—"

That instant, the woman on the left and the man on the right hurled spirals of lightning and ice, which pulsed and staggered as the realm tried to suppress or skew their effects.

Carl jumped and rolled behind a tree to the right. Bailey stood her ground and swept up her cloak. The enchanted scales neutralized the ice shards and deflected a lightning bolt back at the woman with the spear, striking her in the breastplate. She screamed as her muscles seized up; the charge wasn't strong enough to be fatal, but she was incapacitated for the moment. Bailey charged her and the swordsman who'd lied to them as Carl lunged toward the other two.

The werewitch attacked the man with the longsword first since the spearwoman was still recovering. He swept his blade toward her face, and she had to tilt her head back to avoid it. In the same motion, she threw her left-hand sword at him, and it crashed into the faceplate of his helmet.

Then the girl was on him, hooking her elbow around his sword-arm and sticking her foot between his legs to unbalance him. He smashed into the spearwoman as she tried to join the fight. Bailey bashed them both in the heads with her shield, and they went down like dropped sacks of potatoes.

Carl had shoved the other swordsman aside while he

dealt with the guy wielding the flail. The latter swung the pole of his weapon at an angle so the spiked head on its short chain would bypass Carl's mace and strike him in the head.

The scion anticipated that. He blocked the pole with his own weapon, then punched the flail's head with his gauntlet. Steel crunched and Bailey heard Carl gasp in pain, but he yanked the flail out of the man's hands and buffeted him with mace blows.

Bailey retrieved her other sword and pounced on the remaining swordsman, keeping at a distance where she could batter his blade with her shorter weapons. He'd have to make a committed lunge to hit her. Then Carl, having subdued the flail-wielder, flanked the man, and the pair overwhelmed him with a flurry of strikes.

When the last man hit the ground, the horn they'd heard at the beginning of the melee blew again, and the projected image of Malkeg appeared in the center of the clearing.

"Done!" he shouted. "Marvelous job. No one was seriously hurt—well, nothing beyond what a little magic and bed rest can cure—and you used both strategy and tactics. There might be hope for you maggots yet. I only saw a handful of you relying too much on magic. Return to base."

The holograph vanished and a portal opened in its place. Bailey and Carl helped the four they'd beaten to their feet, and all six stepped through, assuming other portals had been conjured for the people elsewhere in the forest.

Carl told the guy with the sword who'd addressed

them, "That was a dirty trick, saying you wanted us not to use magic right as your guys attacked with spells."

The other man shrugged. "You heard Malkeg. No rules except what leads to winning. Too bad we didn't win."

"Yeah, too bad," Bailey agreed.

***

Carl let out a long breath. He was near the end of the table in the same place where he'd sat down next to Bailey during brunch. "Feels good to get out of that stuffy armor. It was chafing my armpit."

Bailey, seated next to him, snorted laughter. "Seconded, and I took the most comfortable option available. I don't want to think about what the guys in full plate went through."

She picked up one of the fluffy bread rolls from her tray and dipped it into the thick chicken soup the mess hall had served for dinner. Their beverage was a crisp and sweet cider again.

The werewitch and the scion spent a few minutes tearing into their food, relishing the boost in energy and feeling of satiation it gave them after their exertions during the mass skirmish. Once they'd eaten two-thirds or so of the meal, they started talking again.

"So," Bailey began, "was that your first time doing that shit? The free-for-all battle in the woods. I get the impression you've been here longer than I have."

Carl guzzled half a cup of cider. "Yes, actually. I've been here for what feels like a week, maybe? It's hard to judge time in the Other."

Bailey nodded. She had noticed the same phenomenon during her previous lengthy sessions of training and combat in the arcane realm.

"But," the scion went on, "this was my first plunge into that particular activity. I think they do it about once a week."

"Gotcha," said the werewitch. "Today's my first full day being here, so it seems like they sure don't waste time. Makes me wonder what the hell else they have in store for us." She mopped up the soup residue in her bowl with what was left of her roll.

Carl's eyes went distant. "There are a wide variety of training methods. That's not in dispute. Expect the unexpected."

Before Bailey could respond, someone came up and stood over them. They both looked up.

Their visitor was a young man even taller and more muscular than Carl, with pale skin, shoulder-length platinum-blond hair, and a broad clean-shaven jaw. He wore a red sleeveless vest and brown trousers.

"Greetings," he opened as he sat down across from the pair. "I am Ragnar the Red-Handed. I've seen the two of you around but have not yet had the chance to speak to you. We've all been busy."

Bailey chuckled. "Ain't that the truth?" She and Carl introduced themselves, and they all shook hands.

Ragnar stuffed a roll in his mouth, chewed, and then remarked, "I suppose you're wondering who I am, aside from my name. I'm a Norse warrior, and it seems I have some godly blood, so the powers that be saw fit to persuade me to come here for training. Likely your own stories are much the same."

Carl leaned back on the bench. "More or less, yes." He and the werewitch gave the capsule versions of their backgrounds.

Bailey asked, "How much godly blood do you have, Ragnar? Are you an outright demigod, or is it more like you're one-sixteenth divine or whatnot?"

Shrugging his heavy shoulders, Ragnar muttered something that started out inaudible and rose to, "I'm not quite sure and it matters not, so there's no point in pressing me on the subject. I have enough divine blood for this place's purposes."

"Fair enough," the werewitch conceded.

Ragnar waved a massive hand. "Anyhow, I saw the results of today's *battle royale.* I've been here for longer than I can remember, long enough that I recall the first one they ever had. They no longer consider it necessary for me to participate in all of them, so they denied me entrance into today's event, but word always spreads when there's a battle composed mostly of new arrivals. People keep an eye on the winners, so I say, well done, the two of you. Beautiful work."

The werewitch and the scion laughed and accepted the Norseman's congratulations, and in the free time allowed to them, they spoke to him about his own life and career. It was obvious to Bailey that he did not come from the modern world. She wondered if after his training was complete, he'd be inserted back into the Viking Age.

Contemplating this further confused her about how time worked in the Other and also made her curious that he knew English, whereas several other trainees had spoken in foreign languages.

"...and so, having vanquished the last of the frost giants on Eysturoy, we returned to Streymoy—that is the most important of the Faroes, you see—and commenced a bout of feasting and drinking that apparently lasted four days. I say *apparently* because someone else had to fill in the details for me later. It was *such* a good feast that I don't remember most of it."

He roared with laughter at his own joke, and his good-natured enthusiasm was so infectious that Bailey and Carl couldn't help laughing, too.

"Ragnar," Bailey stated, "you've had an interesting career, that's for damn sure."

Carl had to agree. "And a longer career than ours, though we've both been around the block a few times, so to speak."

In the short period they'd been speaking to the Norseman, he'd regaled them with tales of hunting monsters and wild beasts, fighting battles and duels, drinking, partying, and rubbing elbows with the gods. He'd seen more violence than Bailey and Carl combined, yet it didn't seem to have affected his jolly demeanor. The culture he came from was...different.

The trainers had no more activities scheduled for them that day. Bailey, Carl, and Ragnar spent some time mingling with other acolytes, drinking a mead-like beverage that got them effectively drunk, talking, joking, and bullshitting. They met a handful of people who seemed worth further interaction, and a couple who seemed like insufferable boors.

The three of them stuck together the whole evening.

Bailey finally retired to her quarters, where Fenris was resting and meditating before the fire, and slipped into bed. An important thought went through her mind:

At least I've made a pair of friends. That definitely helps.

CHAPTER FIVE

Since Roland had spent the night in Portland and it had only been a ninety-minute drive to the northwest of town, he agreed to meet Dante in Leverich Park in Vancouver, Washington, to spare him the final twenty minutes of obnoxious urban driving. Besides, they'd be rambling all over town soon anyway.

"Well," Roland greeted the other wizard as they approached each other across the vibrant emerald grass of the park, "you're looking...about the same, but nothing wrong with that. How goes it?"

Dante snorted and ran the fingers of his right hand through his long blond forelock. "Thanks, I guess. I'm fine. Charlene and I are more or less together now, so that's good. Things in Seattle have been peaceful. It's been a while since I've been to Portland, so this ought to be interesting."

Roland nodded. "Congratulations to the two of you. I thought I saw you guys exchanging an awful lot of 'meaningful glances' before you rambled back to the Puget

Sound, so I'm not shocked. Bailey and I are well. We've gotten to spend time together recently. Not as much as I'd like, but enough."

"Good," Dante acceded. "I think we all deserved a break after...you know, that stuff."

"Aye."

They bullshitted about other things they'd been up to, with Roland bragging about his beautiful new car and claiming that he'd let Bailey defeat him in their informal race since she had, after all, helped him get the Audi nice and cheap. Dante laughed and talked about his and Charlene's experiences with bumping into more and more Weres around town, most of whom wanted to shake their hands.

Neither wizard was an expert on Portland, but they were sufficiently familiar with the local scene to pick out a handful of clubs and daytime hangout spots where they detected the presence of other witches. Walking or taking the bus to get around the city and employing a mixture of casual conversation and the leverage of their growing reputations, they soon picked up the sort of rumors they were looking for.

"Yeah," said a witch named Shana as the three of them lounged in the corner of a combined cafe and bookshop, "last I heard, they were heading out to this shop near Beaverton to pick up spellcraft stuff. That was, like, a week ago. I figured they were busy with other shit, but..." Her voice trailed off, and she looked uncomfortable.

Roland sipped his coffee while Dante did the talking.

"Got it," the younger wizard said. "The person who runs the shop probably would have seen them, right? I'm getting kinda low on a couple things anyway. Do you know where the place is?"

She did, and once they finished their coffee and light lunch, the pair thanked Shana and departed.

Since the shop was located in the western suburbs, they would have to pass Roland's motel room anyway. They stopped there and piled into his Audi, driving themselves rather than bothering with public transportation.

"This way," Roland pointed out, "if something fuckish happens, we can *drive* away at a nice clipping speed rather than having to run and hope we find a taxi or a bus before someone shoots us in the back."

Dante frowned. "Good point. Do you, uh, think it will come to that?"

"Hopefully not," said the older wizard, "but you never know. After some of the crap that's happened this past half-year, I'd say it's better to be prepared for, well, *anything.*"

They found the establishment in an aged brick building, sort of an early strip mall. The shop only occupied the lower east corner. The rest of the structure appeared to be vacant, which was no surprise to Roland. Supernatural folk liked to have extra space adjacent to their businesses in case they needed elbow room for activities they didn't want the general public to know about.

Leaving the Audi parked across the street in the vast lot of a plaza centered around a department store, the two wizards climbed out and strode toward their destination.

Dante looked at the sign out front. "Silver Horizons New Age Shoppe. Sounds unassuming."

Roland smiled. "The proprietor must be the type who

hides in plain sight. In any event, just act like a customer. It's not like there's no reason for us to be there. We're witches. We *need* occult supplies, dammit."

Within, the place was about what they'd expected, with shelves offering a mixture of useless knick-knacks, semi-useful but basic magical paraphernalia, books mostly written by muggles, and the occasional impressive wand. Roland figured that the best stuff was kept in back to protect it from normal people.

After determining that the shop had plenty of white and black candles, Roland approached the counter, with Dante trailing close behind.

The woman there smiled. "Hello. Can I help you find anything?" She was about thirty, with light brown skin paired with light brown hair and green eyes. Roland detected at least one layer of deceptive suggestiveness in her speech. Maybe more.

"Yes," he told her, "I'm looking for red candles, the kind made with authentic red-ochre. They seem to be hard to come by lately, don't they? Do you have any in the back?"

The woman explained she didn't have any on hand but might be able to special-order some after asking around.

"Huh," Roland quipped, furrowing his brow. "A friend of mine was here not too long ago, and I could have sworn she said you carried red-ochre candles."

He gave a name—the name of one of the witches who'd disappeared.

The woman behind the counter betrayed surprise or discomfort, but only slight. Roland had to allow that it might have been because she was miffed that he didn't seem to believe her about the status of her inventory, but it might also have been fear.

"I'm sorry," the proprietor responded. "I don't recognize the name."

Roland and Dante described her and mentioned that the girl had posted a photo of herself to social media just before entering the shop, with its storefront in the background.

When the woman decided that yes, she *had* seen her, Dante asked, "Did she leave any contact information? We want to get in touch with her. To share candles, obviously."

"It would make life easier," Roland agreed.

Now the lady looked actively nervous. She denied having received any contact information from the vanished witch and seemed to be on the verge of asking the two wizards to leave her store.

"Well," Roland began, "we can always call in the—"

Before he could finish, the woman thrust out her hand, and a thick yet soft arcane shield sprouted in Roland's face, muffling him, pushing him back, and blocking both him and Dante off from pursuing her as she turned and fled.

"Shit!" Dante exclaimed. "She's heading upstairs. We can corner her up there."

Roland raised his hands and tore the shield apart with a pair of short plasma blades around his fingers. Then he plunged through the hole, with Dante at his heels.

Behind the counter, a hallway bent toward a staircase. As the two wizards sprinted up it, they saw a door move on the second floor. Roland cleared the landing and yanked it open before it could fall shut, then cursed under his breath.

A woman's leg and foot vanished into a glowing purple gateway in the center of the dark room beyond the door.

He motioned to Dante. "Come on! After her." He ran toward the portal and hurled himself through it.

The wizards emerged only a second before the magical doorway closed behind them. They were standing in a dark forest full of black trees barren of leaves. Overhead, a bone-white moon shone in the dark indigo sky. The witch from the shop was nowhere in sight, but her rustling footfalls sounded ahead and to the right.

Roland set off after her.

Maybe, he reflected, *I'm being too optimistic here, but I ought to be able to catch up with someone who's six inches shorter than I am. Unless of course she pulls out the magical stops to bolster her speed or jumps through another goddamn portal.*

The woman tried no such thing. Instead, as Roland and Dante started to close in, weaving through the tall black trees, she tossed a net of static electricity back over her shoulder.

Roland almost ran into it, but he summoned a curtain of water that neutralized it with sparks and smoke. He threw the whole mass aside and hurtled forward.

Beside him, Dante launched a lance-like blast of sonic percussive force, an attack intended not to kill but to knock the woman over and stun her, make her ripe for capture and questioning. She darted sideways and the projectile hit a tree, blowing half its trunk apart in a shower of wooden fragments.

The running battle continued through the nocturnal forest, the witch trying to disable or confuse her pursuers as they attempted to incapacitate her. Finally, Roland conjured an illusory tree three feet in front of the woman's face when she shot a glance over her shoulder, so that when she looked forward, she was about to run into it and stumbled in shock. Dante hit her with another concussive blast that sent her rolling head over feet in some weedy muck.

The wizards closed in around her sides, Roland conjuring a sword blade of sorcerous plasma to hold at the woman's throat. Dante put his knees on her arms and shoulders, pinning her down.

"All right," Roland grunted, "nice try, but now you need to tell us what the hell's going on. We're not going to kill you, but don't piss us off further."

The witch broke down sobbing, her face turning red. "I'm sorry," she bawled. "I didn't mean to. I didn't want to. I'll tell you. Please don't...don't..."

Dante snapped, "Didn't mean to what?"

Roland drew the arcane blade back by about a foot to help the woman calm down, though he kept it active to be safe. After the witch got hold of herself, she began stammering that she knew they were looking for the missing girl and probably a couple of others as well, but that she wasn't *really* responsible.

The wizards frowned. Roland asked, "What's your name?"

"Megan," the woman said. "Please, I'm being blackmailed. This woman, or creature—I don't think she was human—*made* me do it. I was so scared. This horrible thing under heavy black robes with an insanely powerful magical aura told me to do what she said, or she'd kill me slowly. She made me cast sleeping spells on some of my customers, only real casters, and stand aside when she came to collect them. It wasn't my fault!"

Roland stared at her with a mixture of anger and disgust. "You could have gone to someone equally or more powerful, but instead, you collaborated to save your own hide. That's super admirable. Good job. From the sound of it, this other person, or thing, whatever, is what we're most concerned with."

He glanced at Dante, who nodded. Then he added, "So, cooperate with us, and perhaps we can work out a deal."

"Yes," Megan gasped at once. "Whatever you want. Just protect me from *her*."

Dante rubbed his lips. "*We're* customers of yours, kinda. We could pose as the next victims. When is this witch-creature coming back? Oh, and tell us everything you can remember about her."

The young woman stared into space for a moment before she could speak again. "She came into my shop not long ago," she began, "and I thought she was, you know, an old woman with a health condition or something. She had this old, dry, raspy voice that gave me the chills the first time I heard it, and her limbs seemed extremely long compared to how short and small she was. Her arms were all withered, like a person in their nineties or hundreds, but she moved too fast to be that old."

Roland chewed a lip as he contemplated the shopkeeper's words. The description didn't match anyone or anything he knew or had heard of.

"And," Megan added, beginning to tremble, "her aura. My

goddess, it was so strong and terrible. It reached out for me and smacked me around almost, but the woman only stood there looking at me from under her black hood. I couldn't do anything. I was helpless. I don't even know what she wants with the witches she took as captives. I'm so sorry!"

"Yeah," said Roland. "When will she be back next?"

Megan swallowed. "Tomorrow night."

The wizards looked at each other once more and exchanged nods.

"Then," Roland stated, "we'll be there, so she doesn't leave empty-handed. Now let's get back to your shop. And *don't* try anything."

Bailey jerked herself up into a sitting position and kicked the covers away from her feet, her arms raised and her hands balled into fists. She blinked until she could see, but the only person in her room was Fenris.

A trumpet had blasted once, then twice, while boots stomped through the manor's halls. Voices were shouting in loud, hoarse tones that suggested anger, fear, and serious business in general.

Fenris was half-crouched at the foot of the bed, gazing at the door with narrowed eyes. He glanced at the girl.

"It's an alarm," he explained before she could ask. "Though there does not seem to be any immediate danger. They want everyone to assemble in front of the building at once."

Bailey rolled to her feet, pulled her boots on, ran fingers

through her hair, and splashed water on her face. She was ready.

"All right," she muttered. "Let's go."

The werewitch and the wolf-deity exited the room, joining a procession of bleary-eyed yet concerned-looking trainees who trudged after the valet in his colorful clothes. He nearly deafened them with a further blast of his trumpet.

They formed a mass in the front yard before the manor-barracks, sorting themselves into two long ranks, and whispers went up and down the lines.

Bailey leaned toward a couple of young men talking to the side of her.

"Someone was murdered!" one reported.

The other made a scoffing sound of disbelief. "Who?"

"I don't know yet. Wait, *two* people. They found them just before they woke us up. This whole place is on lockdown. All the trainers and guards and servants are running around the perimeter of the castle to make sure no one gets out and looking for tracks."

Bailey swallowed acrid spit. She wondered who the hell would dare to murder half-divine beings at an academy run by the gods, and her gut clenched as she thought of who the victims might be. She searched the ranks with frantic glances, seeking out Carl and Ragnar.

She saw both of them. Carl was in front of her and six or seven spaces to the left. Ragnar had joined her in the back row, about ten spaces to the right. She sighed in relief, though she hated the thought of anyone having been killed for no reason.

Malkeg Ironfist appeared before them. Improbable as it

seemed, the werewitch was not shocked to see him fully outfitted in plate armor, as he'd been yesterday. He carried his mace rested on his shoulder pauldron.

"Listen up," the man barked. "Since you've probably set to gossiping, yes, there's been a pair of murders." He stated the names of the deceased, but Bailey didn't recognize them.

As he spoke, the valets went down the lines, counting all the trainees to ensure that everyone was present who was supposed to be.

Malkeg went on, "Before you ask, no, we don't know who did it yet, or why. The level of power and skill you all have means that every last one of you is potentially a suspect. However, most of your kind lack subtlety and these were clean, silent kills. Throats cut, minimal sign of struggle, no fucking around. No magic appears to have been used, and no one claims to have heard a thing."

The werewitch's mouth dropped open. She had no idea how such a thing was possible in a place like this. It made no sense.

The trainer continued through teeth gritted in barely suppressed fury, "There's nothing we can do about it yet, and we have a regimen to stick to, so don't anyone get the idea that you're going to be let off easy because of the morning's events. *We* will take care of the murderer. *You* need to focus on what's ahead."

One of the valets came up to Malkeg and informed him that, "Everyone is here except the unfortunate two."

Ironfist moved his head and grunted. "Good."

He looked back at the crowd. "You're all safe for the moment, except from me. If any of you want to try murdering someone, step up and try your hand against the Ironfist. And if, now that we know this is going on, you want to try killing someone else, go for it. See what happens."

No one moved or spoke. Bailey suspected that the murderer, whoever they might be, was a third party, not part of the ranks of trainees, but she had no way of being sure.

Malkeg continued his spiel. "Today, I'm going to run you all through hell. You've allowed an assassin into your midst, and you haven't provided any way of catching the culprit. If you can't manage that, I'm forced to make proper heroes, gods, and goddesses out of you."

The guy next to Bailey muttered, "Great."

One of the valets snapped, "No talking!"

Malkeg ignored the minor incident as though confident that the trainees would receive plenty of punishment soon. "You don't get food today. Not yet. Instead, you're running the gauntlet—a single-style obstacle course, no teaming up this time. Each of you is in it alone. We, the trainers, will attack you in addition to the other things you'll have to deal with."

Bailey had to admit to a morbid curiosity as to what the trainers were capable of. She didn't relish having to fight them on an empty stomach, though.

The armored man before them grinned evilly. "Nothing is forbidden except killing. Fight back against us as best you can. Attacking one another is not only allowed but encouraged. Do whatever you must to win. *Win.* Make it to the end in one piece. You will be ranked according to placement, first to last, and the individual who places last forfeits all meals for the rest of the day."

Well, the werewitch mused, *at least I only have to do better than the absolute worst schmuck here.*

She wanted to do better than that, though. Far better.

"Oh," Malkeg concluded, "and no weapons or armor. Your powers, your skills, and the clothes on your back are all you get. Now move out!" He waved his mace and marched into the inner bailey toward the keep, this time taking them toward another outbuilding where a different portal awaited.

Trainers and valets kept close eyes on the trainees as they marched, single file, into the glimmering doorway. Bailey held her breath, then released it the instant before she stepped into the chamber and through the rippling purple surface.

Bailey jumped as the forest trail before her collapsed, seemingly in slow motion. Her perception and reflexes were so keyed up that she anticipated the pitfall trap before it happened. She soared into the air, using magic to carry her farther since the hole that opened was beyond the distance a mere mortal could have cleared.

She slowed herself down as she reached the far side and landed softly on her feet, then ran on. Somewhere ahead and off to the side, she heard the grunts and shouts of combat between other trainees, or possibly a fight against one of the trainers.

Next she came to a deep chasm whose edges were lined

with strange glowing stones. Approaching the crystals, she felt an inner numbness, like part of her personality was being muffled.

An anti-magic field, she surmised.

The only way across the abyss was over a series of interconnected logs forming a narrow rounded bridge. Bailey could have paused and studied the crystals to learn the holes in their anti-arcane properties, then flown across, but that would have taken time, and she didn't know how far ahead—or behind—she was in the race relative to the others.

She inhaled and plunged onto the logs, swaying with vertigo as her feet struggled for purchase on the curved surface. She forced herself to look straight ahead. Looking down would doom her.

Then she started to slip. Instinctively, she shifted into her wolf form, her body elongating and sprouting fur. Her clothes distended and gained a few rips and tears but stayed on her since she'd regulated the size of her lupine shape to remain within those limits. Her greater strength and agility in wolfen form saved her. Grasping the log with her forelegs, she dragged herself back to the top and center and bounded on, jumping as much as she ran, using her clawed feet and giving herself no time to fall.

Soon she was running through the grass at the other side of the chasm, and she stood up, once again in the shape of a young woman.

Ahead was something like a cave or a ruined building. Before she reached it, a path from elsewhere in the forest intersected the one she was on, and she almost crashed into another pseudo-god. He looked like a wiry man of Asian descent.

Their eyes widened at the unexpected meeting, and the man slashed at Bailey's face with a weak plasma blade, one that would have scalded and temporarily blinded her but not killed or seriously maimed. She fell back, conjuring a shield in time to block his next strike. His speed was incredible.

Rather than try to match him in hand-to-hand combat, Bailey commanded the nearest tree to crash into his midsection, knocking him aside. As the man struggled to his feet, branches and vines and grass grew and twisted around him, imprisoning him there. Bailey surrounded the entire mass with a thick shield.

Then she turned and ran onward. The man would be able to cut or blast his way out in a minute or so, but that was enough time for her to pull ahead.

The stone structure looked like a crude temple or crypt, but it might have been a natural formation. On either side of it, the vegetation was dense, so it would take too long to destroy it. She moved into the black doorway at a trot but had to fall to her knees when the passage narrowed to a tunnel.

There was no light. With her eyes rendered useless, Bailey was forced to rely upon her other senses. She was grateful that as a werewolf, she had a natural advantage over those who came from human stock.

She sensed small changes in the quality of the atmosphere up ahead and heard the way her displacement of dust and space moved the air through gaps or holes.

When one of the openings drew near, she darted a hand

out in front of it and retracted it instantly. Wood, stone, and metal ground as a long object like a spear shot out of the hole.

"Crap," she muttered and crawled under the opening flat on her belly.

There were others, and she didn't know how she avoided being skewered. She conjured a shield around herself, one optimized for deflection rather than absorption, and two of the spears grazed her, only to be knocked off course and broken before they could return to their homes.

Grinning, the girl completed the tunnel and emerged into a short hallway with a rectangle of daylight at the far end. She ran back out into the forest.

It occurred to her that breaking two of the spears would make it easier for anyone who came through the passage behind her to get through in one piece and thereby catch up to her. She dismissed the thought and pressed on.

A short way up the trail, the girl heard the sounds of a fierce struggle going on ahead and to her left. She thought about intervening. The combatants might keep each other distracted, but if one defeated the other, she'd find herself with a new adversary.

With the element of surprise, she might neutralize two opponents at once. She crept through the foliage and looked.

Ragnar was there, his blond mane flying in the breeze as he grappled with a leaner man with short dark hair. The Norseman was bleeding from a wound in the meat of his shoulder, and near the feet of the men lay a woman Bailey didn't know who had a nasty cut to her torso, along with a broken neck. She was dead.

Both men looked up as the werewitch intruded.

"Bailey!" Ragnar shouted. "It's him. He's got to be the killer!" He shoved the other guy away from him.

The girl, her heart pounding, moved toward Ragnar's side. The dark-haired man's head darted around, and he hurled a static-tinged blast of kinetic force at the two of them. Since Ragnar was in front, he took the bulk of the spell and tumbled back into a tree. Bailey, shrugging off the minor effects that got through to her, caught the Viking under his good shoulder and hauled him to his feet.

The other man had fled.

Ragnar grunted, "We have to get him. I don't care what they said about not teaming up!"

"Agreed," said Bailey. "Stopping the murders is more important."

In unison, they broke into a sprint, following the obvious trail left by the suspect. Bailey spared a regretful glance at the dead woman.

The thicket fell away behind them and they entered a grassy sward between two high sheer cliffs, with ruined stone walls here and there to provide obstacles or block routes of escape. The dark-haired man was well ahead of them but seemed to be losing ground.

Someone jumped out from behind a rock protrusion as the pair ran. His forearm struck Bailey in the face and she crashed into the cliff, snarling in pain and anger.

By the time she got her bearings, Ragnar had plowed into the attacker and was punching him in the face and stomach. It looked like he was about to sweep the Norseman's ankles with his foot, so Bailey kicked him in the tail-bone. He yelped and crumpled, and Ragnar threw him aside.

"Come on," the Viking urged, and they continued their pursuit.

At first, they closed the distance, but their quarry managed to speed up and maintain his pace a good hundred yards ahead of them. There was no end to the canyon in sight, only an endless natural corridor. However, the path widened in front of the place where the dark-haired man's feet now struck the earth.

Bailey summoned an inferno of roaring flames to block the suspect's path forward. He staggered to the side of the wider space, then Bailey and Ragnar were on top of him, cornering him against the cliff wall.

"You," the Viking growled, "will pay for what you've done!"

"No!" the man protested. He looked at Bailey while gesturing at Ragnar. "I didn't do anything! *He's* the killer."

Bailey scoffed, thinking of a comment Sheriff Browne back in Greenhearth had once made to her. "If you're innocent, why'd you run away?"

Failing to produce a good answer, the man shrieked and launched a torrent of magic at his pursuers. Bailey shielded herself and Ragnar from most of it, and the Norseman waded straight ahead while the werewitch moved in from the side.

Bailey launched a narrow bolt of concussive energy that struck the man on the hip. He stumbled to his knees, and his spells died.

"Prove it," Bailey demanded, moving closer to him and

conjuring a red plasma sword to hold near his face. "If Ragnar's guilty, what's the evidence?"

The man's eyes rolled up and his mouth opened and shut, but no sound came out. He cried out again, and Bailey was swept off her feet by an icy whirlwind that tossed her into the grass across the canyon. Then the man was running through the dying fire, shielding himself from its heat.

Ragnar charged after him, jumping over the flames. He called back over his shoulder, "I can't wait for you. He must not get away. Catch up if you can."

The werewitch climbed to her feet, gritting her teeth at the punishment of all the blows and tossings-around she'd taken, and stared after the two dwindling forms.

"What the *fuck* is going on here?"

Roland lay on the floor of the side storeroom, Dante beside him, in a fetal position with his hands behind his back. They'd wound ropes and cords around themselves to create the illusion of being bound, but of course, they were not. The cords would fall away with a sharp tug. They feigned unconsciousness, but both were wide awake.

Night had fallen an hour ago. They'd been lying here ever since, hoping the witch-creature arrived sooner rather than later.

It's been long enough at this point, Roland thought, *that by the time we spring up, we're going to be stiff as all hell. Maybe this wasn't such a good idea.*

Through the intercom, Megan's voice hissed, "Someone's here! I think it's her. I'm going to let them in."

Roland flicked his eyes toward Dante, who matched his gaze and responded to it with a barely perceptible nod.

The shopkeeper's footsteps moved across the floor outside and the front door opened. They heard light footsteps, along with the swish of long robes. Somehow, hearing that sound, Roland decided he would have imagined a figure in a hooded black robe even if Megan hadn't described her visitor that way.

The storeroom door opened. "Here you go," said Megan. "They're sedated. No problems, right?"

Roland's gut tingled. *She sounds nervous. The witch might suspect something, but then again, Megan seemed so terrified of her that she's probably always nervous.*

A voice replied, "Good." It sounded as though it had been carved with a razor from the lungs of a mummified corpse. Roland had to exert tremendous willpower to keep from shuddering.

He felt rather than saw the creature's eyes moving over them. "I don't recognize this one," she rasped, seeming to indicate Dante. Then her gaze moved to Roland, and wind hissed between her teeth. "But I know him! It's Roland. How did you manage to subdue him? And where is Bailey?"

Oh, shit. Roland groaned inwardly. They hadn't planned for the contingency of the mysterious witch *knowing* him. He wondered if she was an agent of the Venatori.

"What?" Megan gasped. "Who? I don't know who that is, and I just gave him a drink. He didn't suspect anything."

"*Bullshit!*" the hideous voice retorted. "Don't lie to me. If you know anything about Bailey or where she is, tell me now!"

The shopkeeper stammered in panic. Roland considered jumping up to attack but decided against it. If he and Dante ended up killing the creature, they'd lose their chance to find out where the missing witches had been taken.

Then he felt powerful magic being employed. Megan's gibbering fell silent as the crone cast a truth-saying spell on her. She rasped, "Tell me everything you know."

The young woman replied in a slurred monotone, "Nothing. I do not know who Bailey is."

A noise that was half-snarl, half-gurgle answered her. "Fine! Obviously you don't. You don't realize what you have here. I've been trying to get my hands on this man for a long time, and at last, I have. Say nothing, and await my next instructions."

Megan stepped back as the small robed figure came into the room and opened a warped-looking portal. Roland wondered where it led.

The crone ground out, "This will be an interesting night. Heh, heh."

The wizards felt themselves rising from the floor as the witch-creature levitated them and hurled them into the gateway, where dizzying cold and flashing purple light engulfed them.

CHAPTER SIX

Bailey ran up hills, through tangles of jungle, and over rocky cliffs and badlands. Spring-loaded traps, nets, and more pitfalls challenged her, but she evaded them all. Her blood pounded in her skull. Tiredness threatened to overwhelm her, particularly since she felt nauseated from lack of food.

But she pressed on. Here and there, she caught glimpses of Ragnar and the man he followed. Other times they vanished into the wilderness ahead of her.

At one point, an athletic-looking black girl bowled into her from the side and attempted to take her out of the race. Bailey saw her shielding her head and torso, so she launched a lightning bolt at the girl's feet, shocking her into immobility, then sinking her chest-deep into a conjured mudhole.

Leaving the young woman to figure out how to free herself, the werewitch continued.

Soon after, she spied a tall, broad-shouldered figure with long platinum hair standing in a clearing beyond a wooded slope. Jogging between the leafy branches, she emerged ready to greet Ragnar, then froze, gasping.

The Norseman stood over the body of the dark-haired man, who lay crumpled on the ground with his head bashed in. A bloody rock rested at his side. Ragnar breathed heavily after the fight.

"Shit, Ragnar," Bailey exclaimed. "What the hell happened?"

He looked up, regarding her with a steely gaze. "I caught him, and we fought. He refused to surrender, so I had no choice but to put him down to protect the others." He stood up straight and paused. "But I heard what he said to you, and I can see how this might look suspicious."

She squirmed in place. "It would have been better if you'd captured him alive," she muttered.

Ragnar growled, "If you believe I am the killer, you'd be justified in putting *me* down, would you not?" Slowly, he turned around, exposing his vulnerable back.

Bailey stared at her new friend. She'd known him for less than a full day. Truly, there wasn't much to suggest she ought to trust him any more than the man who lay dead at his feet. And yet...

"No," she stated. "I'm not going to shoot you in the back, Ragnar. I don't think you're the murderer, and if by some chance you are, they'll catch you anyway. Still, we might have trouble explaining why this guy's dead."

Ragnar shrugged. "I appreciate your trust, but it was foolish of you not to have at least knocked me out."

Before she could ask him what he meant, a twist of his finger conjured a storm cloud that engulfed her and threw her back while invisible hands punched her stomach and slapped her face.

He ran off as the cloud bore her backward. "*Oof!* Ragnar! What the goddamn hell..."

"We're still in competition!" He laughed. "And the race is not yet over!"

Bailey surrounded her body with a shield of spiky arcane essence that blocked the unseen fists and tore the cloud apart. It dissipated and she dropped to her feet, dusting herself off and cursing her stupidity. She should have known that the jovial, macho Norseman would not forget about the competition for an instant.

As she set off, summoning a second wind for the final exertions of the race, her gaze lingered on the dead man in the clearing. She hoped he *was* the murderer since if so, it meant the danger was past. The trainers could retrieve his body later.

What remained of the course was perhaps one-fifth the length of what she'd been through thus far, though it took all her strength to make it to the end. She evaded three more traps and defeated one more contestant, a burly man who appeared to be in his thirties, before the finish line hove into sight at last.

The line was drawn across an open gap in the dense woods at the end of the trail. She saw and heard people bustling beyond, but it was hard to tell how many. She hadn't seen Ragnar since he'd run off, so she was almost positive that the best she could hope for was second place. She knew she was far from last. She'd left too many others behind her for that to be a possibility.

Bailey dashed across into an open field, then slowed her

pace until she came to a stop, bending over with hands on her knees to gulp in air. Malkeg, standing beside the finish line, barked, "Fourth!"

Fourth? her mind echoed. *Not what I'd hoped for, but could be far worse.*

Looking up, she saw Ragnar and Carl and learned they had placed second and third respectively. She hadn't seen Carl at all, so he must have passed her via a different route.

"Bailey," Carl greeted her. "You didn't do badly. Most of the trainees are still bumbling around out there."

"Thanks," she replied.

Ragnar, despite his impressive showing, looked disgruntled. "I should have placed first," he opined. "But I suppose this fellow was the better man."

Following his gaze, Bailey took in the winner. She vaguely recalled seeing him around but hadn't particularly noticed him until now.

He was approximately the same age as she was, mid-twenties, of average height but in excellent physical condition with a leanly-muscled runner's body beneath his simple modern clothes. He had wavy medium-length hair, the color of which was in the limbo between dark blond, light brown, and red.

"Hello," he greeted her in a nondescript bari-tenor voice, "I'm Ethan. Looks like I made it out in front. Anyway, they've opened a portal for us to head back, so I think I'll do so." He shrugged and walked off, then strolled through the purple gateway at the other end of the field.

The girl watched him go. Something about him seemed "off" to her, but she couldn't place what it was.

She turned her eyes to Ragnar and he nodded at

Malkeg, who was watching as the fifth and sixth of the trainees crossed the finish line. When he was done, the pair approached him.

"What?" the man demanded.

Ragnar spoke first. "We caught the murderer." Bailey confirmed most of the details of his brief story.

Malkeg silenced them in the middle of the tale with a sharp wave of his hand. "We know he's dead. We found the body moments before you finished the course. From what we know of that man, weighed against the investigation so far, there's no reason to suspect he was our assassin. We're curious, Ragnar, why you had to kill him."

The Norseman bristled, and Bailey interceded on his behalf. "He was threatening us," she pointed out. "I tried to get him to come along quietly and answer some questions, but he kept tossing lethal magic and running away, not trying to discuss anything. Seemed suspicious as hell, if you ask me." She swallowed and decided to say what had to be said. "He accused Ragnar of being the killer instead but didn't offer any evidence, so I—"

"*Be quiet,*" Malkeg snapped as Ragnar glared at her with a mixture of fury and hurt. The trainer went on, "Idle speculation is of no help to us. Ragnar, tell me again what happened from the beginning. Did you *see* the man murder that girl?"

"No." He grunted. "But he was leaning over her, and there was no sign of anyone else around."

Ironfist growled. "Right. Just as we figured—both of you stumbled onto the body within seconds of each other, and like the hotheaded morons you are, blamed each other. Because neither of you could think like rational beings, one of you is dead, and we'll have to produce explanations for the bereaved. Good fucking job!"

The Viking lowered his face toward the ground, looking abashed and uncertain for the first time.

"More likely," Malkeg added, "while you two were fighting, the real assailant got away and is still at large. Get out of here. Eat and drink something to clear your thick heads. We will continue the investigation while trying to manage all your foot-dragging friends." He jabbed his elbow at the portal.

Bailey and Ragnar strode in the direction the man had indicated, collecting Carl on their way.

"I," Ragnar began, "I did not think of it that way. I would not have killed an innocent man if I'd known. Why did he act that way?" His grief and remorse, like all his emotions, were blatant and theatrical.

Bailey put a hand on his massive shoulder. "We both made a mistake," she acknowledged, "but it's true, that guy should have said or done something different if he was innocent."

Carl chimed in with, "There's nothing we can do now. It was a tragic accident. We need rest and nourishment. Maybe they should have allowed us breakfast before they tossed us into such a stressful situation."

Arm in arm, the three friends walked through the portal.

Roland had feared they might end up in some awful, hellish plane, but the crone's gateway took them to a fairly standard stretch of the Other. It was not a pleasant domain, but he was used to it. Dim purplish-gray light filtered down from a sky of deep violet, and sporadic black trees rose from the marshy earth with its pale, colorless grasses and eerie white mists.

As the witch-creature lowered him and Dante to the ground, no other people or entities were in sight. They were alone in the desolation.

Out of half-lidded eyes, still feigning unconsciousness, Roland watched as their kidnapper raised her gnarled and scrawny hands and drew the black hood away from her face. What he saw was as bad as he'd expected.

The woman, or whatever she was, looked as though she were at least a hundred and twenty years old, perhaps more like five hundred and twenty. Her features were distorted and emaciated, at once withered and mushy. Her skin was the color of ashes, and she resembled no one in particular. Sparse stringy white hair grew from her scalp and fell to her shoulders.

She took a step forward and kicked Roland in the stomach with surprising strength and force. "Wake up!" she snarled. "Have a look and tell me if I look familiar, Roland."

The wizard sprang to his feet, using subtle magic to augment his speed and smooth over the muscular stiffness he'd acquired. In the blink of an eye, he held a sizzling blade of green plasma beside her throat. Dante had jumped up also and stood ready for a fight.

Roland stated, "I don't recognize you, and I don't care. Where are the witches you took? Tell us!"

The crone stared at him as if he was stupid and made an ugly snorting noise. "Too late for that. They're gone. I drained them to restore myself. It's taking too fucking long, though."

She talks like a present-day American, the wizard observed, *which pretty much rules out her being an elderly Venatori operative. Who is she, then?*

Dante gulped as the reality sunk in; the people they'd been searching for were dead.

Roland's lips drew back from his teeth. "Restore yourself from *what?* Who and what are you?"

The creature grinned, and the sight sent chills through Roland's vertebrae.

"You always were kinda stupid," she sneered. "You would have recognized me back when everyone called me *Caldoria McCluskey!*"

The wizard blinked. "Callie? I thought you were—"

"*Dead?* Yeah, no shit!" the witch shot back. "I was. The Venatori fed me to cave wraiths. Then they came back and tried to revive me as part of their stupid scheme to kill Bailey before she destroyed their goddess and screwed everything up. They forgot about me, but I haven't forgotten *anything.*"

Roland tried not to quiver with dread and loathing. In addition to Callie's new and horrible appearance, the thought of her, of all people, becoming a lich was beyond disturbing. In some ways, she had been the worst of the trio centered around Shannon DiGrezza, though all three sorceresses had had an unhealthy obsession with him and his "seed" for far too long.

"I started," Callie went on, "by drawing off the magic of the Venatori who came back here. After they left, I sucked the life out of other witches. I got more power from them than I've ever had before, but it's taking forever to restore my *life*. I always wanted your body," she cackled, "and now you're in my clutches. I'm gonna have it, but in a different way. Ironic."

The wizard took one step back but did not lower his blade. "My body is nowhere near your crusty-ass clutches, and since you're technically dead already, you're about to get the proper dust-to-dust treatment. Fuck off, Callie."

Light and force exploded across the bog as Roland drove his plasma sword toward the witch's face, protecting himself with a thick arcane shield that blocked the wave of boiling lava she hurled at him. He left a space open at her side for Dante to flank her.

The other wizard tried to send a lightning bolt through the gap, but Callie blocked it with a shield of her own and waved a bony arm, sending both young men hurtling back through the air in different directions.

"Ha, ha! You guys completely *suck!*"

In midair, Roland summoned a rain of hail and fire to pin the witch down from above while also shaking the ground with a minor earthquake. It was enough to disorient her and prevent her from finishing them off.

He floated toward Dante and stopped him from falling. The younger wizard must not have known how to fly.

"Holy crap!" Dante cried. "How are you doing that? And she's like, about as powerful as the goddamn Dreadknights were."

Clusters of blue plasma spears streaked toward them while they floated downward and away to seek shelter amidst a copse of dead trees.

"Yeah," Roland agreed. "She did say she got a power

boost from the witches she drained. Listen, instead of fighting fire with fire, let's lead her on a chase. She'll tire faster with her body in the condition it's in."

Dante nodded. He and the other man landed, and the black shape of Caldoria in her billowing robes moved closer. They bolted into the woods.

The witch screamed, "Pussies! You're afraid to fight me? You won't get away!"

The ground trembled, and trees fell over as blasts of magic tore the forest away behind them. Roland conjured a thick moving shield at their backs and felt the massive force of the crone's attacks strain it nearly to breaking point within seconds.

Dante enacted a spell that shifted the lay of the land so the flat area before them sloped upwards. The two wizards, still with bodies in their twenties, ascended it easily, but the crone would have trouble, even with her arcane might.

The running battle wove its way through the boggy wasteland, with Roland and Dante keeping far enough ahead to entice Callie to follow, but not allow her to catch them. They fought defensively as waves of her terrible power were flung at them.

As time went on, the pair found that they kept having to pause and wait for their pursuer to catch up. During one such break, Roland, breathing heavily, turned to his friend.

"Callie was always pretty stupid," he observed, "but she might figure out what we're up to and give up the chase. I think it's time to engage."

"Sure," the other agreed. He grimaced as he flicked his hair. "I can't believe you *know* her, though."

Roland turned away and scanned the wooded slope for the witch. "It's a long story. Shit, there she is."

The squat black-clad shape moved out from between the trees, stumbling as if drunk and resting against trunks every fifteen or twenty steps. The sight was pitiful, comical, and encouraging all at once.

Callie gasped, "There! You...get back...here!" She could hardly speak.

Roland conjured a solid wall of shield material in front of them, then encased both their bodies in shield-armor to be safe. It was all that saved them from the devastating explosion the witch conjured, which drove them reeling apart from sheer physics and reduced a full acre of forest to ash.

Then the wizards attacked. At first, the crone blocked or redirected their projectiles and resisted their enchantments, but she seemed slower and clumsier, as though her mind could not keep up with the exhaustion of her body.

Finally, Dante stripped away her wavering shields and hurled her into a fat tree, knocking her unconscious.

Roland stepped in front of the wasted figure. "Sorry, Callie, but the changes you've gone through lately made you into an even worse person, amazingly. Goodbye."

His hand shot out, and a greenish-white spiral beam of arcanoplasm, electricity, and molten metal struck the crone square in the chest. Coming to at the last instant, she screamed as her body sparked, smoked, and disintegrated into a pile of dust. The burning black robe fluttered to the ground.

Then a breeze came up, stirring the dust and carrying it away through the woods.

"I'll be back," a faint voice whispered. *"I'll...be...back..."*

Roland exhaled and turned away. "No, she won't."

Dante frowned. "Are you sure? You destroyed her, but there was magic going on with her that I'm not familiar with."

"Yeah," Roland replied. He was not a hundred percent certain, but ninety-nine percent was close enough. "She's dust. No more local witches getting drained."

It occurred to both, though, that they'd failed to save the people who'd been taken. More lives had been lost at a time when the Pacific Northwest's paranormal community was just starting to emerge from the trauma of the war against the Venatori. The pair stood in dejected silence.

Dante commented, "I knew one of them—that girl Renee. Not very well, but still. She's gone."

"I'm sorry to hear that." Roland recalled a time when Callie, for all her obnoxiousness, had not been a deadly and monstrous enemy. He'd lost her, too. "Well, at least we avenged them and stopped the problem at its source. That will have to be good enough."

CHAPTER SEVEN

The mess hall served mead that evening. It came as a relief, but Bailey was starting to wonder if it might have been a mistake.

The werewitch was dejected. Ragnar's depression was rubbing off on her, and the alcohol wasn't helping.

"How?" the Norseman wailed, wringing his hands over the wooden table. His eyes were wet and shiny. "How could I have made such a foolish error? How could I have lost my head to such an extent? Yes, I could offer a payment of *weregild* to his family, but will that be enough? Will it redeem the shame I've brought upon myself or replace the dreams his loved ones held for him?"

He'd barely eaten, though he had downed four cups of mead. Bailey wondered why the servers weren't enforcing a drink limit. She was on the verge of cutting him off from further intoxication herself.

Carl put a hand atop Ragnar's. "Hey, now. It was a terrible thing, but accidents do happen, and you thought you were doing right. We're all under a lot of strain, and it's much worse with a murderer on the loose."

Bailey wolfed down some of the chicken and dumplings the facility had served for supper, wanting to help Ragnar but knowing he would have to help himself if he wanted to get through this.

"Many men and monsters have I killed," the Viking continued. "But there was cause in each case. I had always thought myself better than this. An innocent man has died! If such a thing can happen, do I truly deserve the power of the gods? The responsibility?"

The werewitch swallowed her food and told him, "We've all fucked up in pretty bad ways, Ragnar. There are things I wish I could go back and undo, but I don't think even the gods have *that* power."

The Norseman cursed in a language Bailey didn't recognize—perhaps Old Icelandic?—and smacked his huge hands on the wooden surface, then rose suddenly from the bench and stomped into the smoky gloom beyond the kitchen.

Bailey and Carl exchanged glances. The scion asked, "Should we go after him? I'm worried."

The werewitch pursed her lips. "I don't think so. He's the emotional type, but he's tough. He needs to mope for a while and get this all out of his system. We'll see how he's doing in the morning."

Carl agreed, and they ate in silence for a bit before resuming their conversation, though they steered it toward more pleasant matters.

"That guy Ethan," Bailey started. "Nice hair, but he seemed awfully, uh, nonchalant about winning, like he just stumbled into it and it was no big deal. I think that might be the worst false modesty I've ever seen."

Carl snickered. "Yeah, something like that. I guess it's better than if he'd been an egotistical prick about it, but still. Oh, do you know who came in last? I feel bad for them whoever they were, but rules are rules."

Bailey shrugged. "I didn't inquire. Not anyone I know. They'll live, though, as long as we get a proper breakfast tomorrow."

Feeling mischievous, they glanced at the trainees eating and drinking in the hall, speculating who the loser had been and laughing like dumb schoolgirls. Soon they turned to trying to guess what each person's divine background and portfolio might be.

Bailey pointed at a hugely fat trainee who was wolfing down his third plate of dinner. "Look at that guy there. What do you suppose his power is? A hollow leg with a portal at the bottom? Must be the son of the god of all four seasonal feasts."

Carl chuckled, half-embarrassed at himself, and Bailey blushed as well. Normally she didn't go around mocking people's looks, but right now, she felt like *any* levity would be healthy, including the mean-spirited variety.

"Or her," the scion remarked, gesturing at a woman whose hair was styled in a mohawk-ponytail hybrid like the crest of a Roman centurion's helmet. "The demigoddess of hairspray. Sponsored by...shit, I don't know any hairspray brands offhand. I never use that crap."

Bailey cracked up. "Yeah, we got some interesting characters here." She took another swig of mead. "Like, in all fairness, I guess I'd be the goddess of muddy pickup trucks."

They spouted further rounds of jokes, challenging each other to come up with the most creatively offensive bullshit until a small crowd gathered around them: five young men, and they looked angry.

Bailey sighed. "I have a history of problems of this particular sort when I'm in an establishment that serves alcohol," she confided to Carl as though their new visitors couldn't hear them.

"Hey!" the apparent leader of the group growled. "We heard what you said. My girlfriend doesn't even use hairspray!"

The werewitch spread her hands. "Makes it all the more impressive she can maintain that hairstyle, then."

"Shut up!" one of the others bellowed.

Carl narrowed his eyes. "Don't talk to her like that. We're just joking around. Nothing worth getting seriously antagonistic over, you know."

Apparently, they didn't know since they continued to argue and threaten. Things were teetering on the brink of violence, but the gang refused to make the first move.

Bailey stood up. "For fuck's sake. If you're going to surround us and act all tough, you can't drag out the shit-talking phase indefinitely like a bunch of chimpanzees hooting at each other. You either got to make your move or leave. Which is it gonna be?"

Carl stood up too.

The leader trembled with indignation. "No," he retorted, "you started it, so *you* leave." Clearly, he hadn't gotten the message.

"Right." Bailey nodded and punched him in the jaw. He staggered back, sputtering and flailing his limbs.

The other four piled into her and the scion, and their table was kicked over. Mead cups crashed to the floor, and thrashing bodies struggled.

Exclamations, oaths, curses, and whoops of delighted amusement went up from the other trainees nearest them. Those on the other side of the mess hall did not bother to investigate. They were too tired to care about anything that didn't directly affect them right now.

Bailey braced herself against one of the posts holding up the hall's roof and kicked with both legs, taking one of the guys full in the chest and knocking the wind out of him. He groaned and crumpled, replaced immediately by a bald-pated bruiser who directed a massive punch at her. She spun aside and the man's fist smashed into the pillar, splintering the wood.

Meanwhile, Carl had put the guy closest to him in a headlock and successfully used him as a human shield, so his stomach absorbed a punch from the fifth man. He tossed his captive aside and grappled with the other attacker, the two struggling over the lumber of the fallen table.

In another minute, it was over. Three of the gang lay incapacitated, and the remaining two were in a stalemate with Bailey and Carl. All four of those still on their feet had bruises, black eyes, bloody lips, and lightly twisted limbs. No one was badly injured, but they knew they'd been in a fight.

Bailey laughed all of a sudden, and the men looked at her oddly. "You know," she quipped, "I'm used to fighting mortals, humans mainly. I forgot you guys are better quali-fied to put up a proper tussle. Let's just say I'm sorry I shot my mouth off and have another drink. I think we all needed to blow off some steam."

Carl laughed too, hearing that, and grudgingly, the two men opposite them nodded. They shook hands, helped their friends up, and righted the table as well.

Bailey spied the leader's mohawked girlfriend staring at her. "Sorry," she called.

One of the trainers, not Malkeg but another whose name the werewitch didn't know, ducked under the heavy hangings that passed for walls and glared around. "What happened?" he demanded.

Carl shrugged. "Someone tripped over the table leg and spilled the food. We cleaned it up, though. May we have a second helping?"

<hr>

"Fenris."

The wolf-god looked up. He'd been sitting cross-legged in front of the fireplace and gazing into the flames as though meditating. "Yes?"

Bailey walked over and sat down on the bearskin rug next to him. "Rough day," she began. "Got into the closest thing we have here to a bar brawl. Nothing serious, though. What happened earlier was..." She swallowed spit as her voice trailed off.

Fenris waited for her to find her tongue. When she did, rather than tell him about Ragnar's manslaughter incident, she asked, "Did they find out anything more about the murders?"

The deity shook his head. "Not really, no. A few tracks, subtle and slight, leading away from where the bodies were found, but whoever is responsible is skilled enough that they couldn't uncover much. I heard there were further deaths on the obstacle course."

She nodded. "Yeah, you could say that."

Inhaling, she told him the whole story, ending with how despondent Ragnar had been over it at the end of the day.

Fenris paused to digest her words before he replied, "First of all, the accident was highly unfortunate. It sounds like Ragnar is sincere in his repentance, but to have made such an error suggests that he might not possess the self-control for full godhood. But his blunder is not the biggest issue here; the murders are."

"I'll second that," Bailey murmured.

"I had wondered how long it would take," the tall shaman went on, "before someone resorted to this."

The girl was puzzled. "What do you mean?"

Fenris grimaced. "It is not uncommon for interested parties and higher powers to take out other proto-gods and pseudo-gods during training. It represents a period of volatility and vulnerability when 'accidents' can happen. It's a prime opportunity for those who don't wish to be challenged to remove potential competition before they have to deal with it openly."

The fire seemed darker. "I see," Bailey said.

"It is frowned upon, but in a way, it is expected in much the same way that, say, steroid use among professional athletes is expected. No matter how much noise the trainers make about wanting control of the situation they preside over, or how much the families grieve and complain, there are often assassinations. Even the gods take cheap shots at one another when they can, you see."

There was an underlying bitterness in his tone, and Bailey thought back to the frigid and uncomfortable discussion with the other deities in the conclave.

Fenris turned his head and looked into the werewitch's eyes. "Trust no one, Bailey. Be vigilant, and don't give too much of yourself away or leave yourself open. Watch your back. If things get out of hand and you are in serious danger, I will pull you out of this place, conventions be damned."

"Can you *do* that? Or is there a covenant against it, too?" She wasn't being sarcastic; she was curious to know how the intricate politics of the divine realms affected her fate, and by extension, the fates of all mortals.

Her mentor didn't answer directly. "This is a legitimate form of training," he explained, "but it's also a formality to placate and pacify the other deities. At the end of the day, you have the power of a goddess, yet you are my apprentice. You've achieved full shamanhood and more, but you still operate under my proverbial wing. That means I'm responsible for you. For all your progress, you are yet a neophyte. I will complete your instruction myself, teaching you to be a goddess alone if I must."

She put a hand on his arm. "Thank you. Let's hope that won't be necessary."

"We shall see," he rumbled. "There is one thing, however, that we ought to do tonight. I'd been debating whether to teach it to you yet, but I think the time has come."

"Okay," she agreed. "You've always been a good teacher, and I feel more alert than I would have guessed for being tired as hell and a little drunk."

He smiled. "You have been a good student. What we will learn now is how you can gain greater control over your new, divine powers. Part of that will be done via opening a channel between us."

Hearing that, the werewitch thought back to the titanic battle against Aradia, whom she had destroyed in part by using herself as a conduit through which the evil goddess' essence and might had bled out.

Fenris went on, "Some of this will be a review of things you already know but which are important enough that you'll benefit from having them fresh in mind. Other lessons will be refinements. You've learned the foundations but could stand further lessons on the details and specifics. And some will be entirely new to you, but it's all necessary and helpful. Once more, you must adapt or fail."

"Well," she remarked, "I was never a fan of failing. Adaptation it is."

"Good." The wolf-father raised a hand. "As with your confrontation with the Venatori's patron, I want you to open a channel between you and me, but this will be different. You won't be using me as an anchor or reservoir as you did then, nor will you be spilling my powers out as you did to Aradia. It will be more like that time when you and Roland and I established a circuit and passed a bolt of electricity around."

She nodded. "Makes sense, I think." She touched the

palm of her hand to his, closed her eyes, and concentrated on his vast store of magic, as well as the almost-as-vast supply within herself, dormant though most of it was.

Fenris continued his explanation. "This will help you with trading energy between beings of immense power. You will gain a better understanding of the subtler sorts of magic that might be enacted with your new abilities despite the sheer brute force you possess. And choice control, the same lucid-mindedness and emotional self-discipline that any mere human can and ought to learn, which you must cultivate while channeling and partaking of essences that no mortal ever has to deal with."

Bailey imagined a rope or tube extending from her forehead and linking to Fenris's chest. Then she pictured herself opening a door or cabinet and set water, fire, electricity flowing between them.

Thus the conduit was established. As during the final struggle against the Venatori, she felt his essence, coldly imposing and yet wise and sturdy and patient.

This time she also sensed a simmering rage in him, but it was far beneath the surface of his consciousness, and she tried not to focus on it. He must have still been mad at his sister and the other deities of the council.

She knew Fenris felt her, and the residual power stolen from Aradia. "Good," he stated. "You are off to a smooth start. Now we will begin basic exercises in trading spells in the sub-universes that are contained within our bodies. As these grow in intensity, you will be confronted by scenarios where you must quickly make difficult choices without blind emotion interfering in your judgment."

"I understand," she assured him.

"The training here," he went on, waving his hand to indicate he meant the castle and its grounds, "is more about stress response. The acolytes are shuffled between situations of combat, physical strain, and circumstances meant to induce panic. The idea is to test their endurance in ways that teach them not to respond to any difficulty with massive explosions of destructive power or take slights personally, or do anything rash or stupid. Choice control, as it's called. That is a type of control that can ultimately come only from within you, Bailey."

Her nostrils flared as she breathed in, and they began what promised to be a long night.

/

CHAPTER EIGHT

Two more people were murdered overnight.

Once again the trainers and valets had stormed through the halls, shouting and blowing trumpets, commanding everyone to rise and assemble at once in the front yard before the manor.

They'd all done so, and Malkeg presented himself before the lines of the trainees, looking more enraged than usual. "Right," he growled. "You know what's going on. The killer among us has claimed another pair of victims despite our best efforts to root him or her out, not to mention how much we've beefed up security. If anyone knows *anything* that might point us in the direction of this son of a bitch, now is the time to tell us."

Bailey knew nothing except what she'd told them yesterday. No one else spoke either; the moods of the trainees were hushed, fearful, angry, and disgusted.

"Right," the Ironfist barked. "If you can't help, stay out of the way. Here's how things are going to work. You will all be permitted to eat breakfast in the mess hall, then you will be put in quarantine in your rooms. You are to remain there until given permission to emerge. That will be far safer than throwing you into situations where we can't watch you constantly. If the murderer tries anything, they'll run afoul of us very quickly. Everyone got that?"

They all yelled back that they did. A few made half-assed moping sounds at the notion of being confined to their quarters, but given the seriousness of the situation, nobody openly protested.

Malkeg grunted, "So be it, then. March to the mess hall. Eat. Don't waste time!"

They turned in unison and, keeping roughly in a formation of two long lines, moved out to take their meals.

Bailey collected a heaping plate of eggs, potato hash, and mixed fruit, combined with a cup of good strong tea with honey. She carried it back to the same end of the same table she'd used thus far, and Carl and Ragnar joined her a moment later.

"Morning," Carl greeted them. "Not sure if it's 'good,' though."

Ragnar grunted. "Could be worse. We are all alive, and they prepared a fine and proper meal for us."

Bailey smiled. "That's the truth. I haven't had a breakfast this size in quite some time."

She noticed that Ragnar seemed to be in better spirits than he'd been last night. There was still a gloomy gruffness to his demeanor, but he'd slept off all the mead he'd drunk, and the worst of his angst appeared to have dissipated along with the alcohol.

Carl noticed, too. "You're feeling better?"

"Somewhat," the Norseman replied. "My failure

still…disturbs me, but the skein of Fate, once woven, cannot be unwoven. What's done is done. I will make amends as well as I can and otherwise forge ahead."

Bailey patted his shoulder. "Good man. That's the best way to approach it, I'd say. We'll all have time to reflect on shit if they're locking us in our damn rooms. At least it means they ought to be able to catch the bastard."

Ragnar glowered, and violence simmered beneath the surface of his mind. "Would that I could be the one to catch him," he growled.

The dark-faced scion gave the Viking a concerned frown. "Understandable sentiment, but don't do anything hasty for your own sake."

Ragnar muttered to himself and tore into his food.

Moments later, five guys strode up to their table. At first, Bailey thought they were the same quintet she and Carl had tangled with last night, but she didn't recognize them.

"Morning," she said. "Can we help you, gentlemen?"

They ignored her. One of them planted a hard shove on Ragnar's shoulder, causing him to spill a forkful of eggs and potatoes on the table. The Norseman turned around slowly, his eyes blazing.

"You," said one of the men, a lean, olive-hued individual with a black ponytail. "The man you killed yesterday, supposedly by accident? His name was Nikos, and he was our friend."

Bailey and Carl watched, tense and alert, but allowed Ragnar to speak for himself.

"It was an accident," the Viking growled. "My remorse

is great, and I'll pay *weregild* to his family. I shall also help find the real murderer."

The leader of the hostile group snorted. "Pay? Oh, and wasn't there a dead woman found at your feet? Seems pretty fucking suspicious, doesn't it?"

Ragnar stood up with enough speed and force to knock over the bench he'd been sitting on and spun to face the group. "You would destroy this fine dining hall?" he asked. "Or should we take this outside?"

The olive-skinned man replied, "No magic. Fists and muscle only. Seems fair, right?"

Bailey and Carl stood up. "Just to be clear," the were-witch interjected, "we think five against three is a lot fairer than five against one. Right?"

One of the group threw a piece of wood at Carl's head, probably to take him out of the fight before it began, but it missed. Then pandemonium erupted. The trio piled into the quintet, and the first three of the dead man's friends hit the floor as Bailey, Carl, and Ragnar moved in to thrash the remaining two.

Light filtered into the hall and boots stomped. Malkeg and two other trainers had appeared.

"*Hey!*" the plate-armored man bellowed, "Knock it off! I said, break it up, fuckheads!"

The scuffle ended as the three trainers interposed themselves and restrained Ragnar and the ponytailed leader of the gang, who were still trying to hurl themselves against one another. The others relaxed and stepped back.

Malkeg said to the two belligerents, "You two, go back to your rooms at once. The rest of you can finish your breakfasts, but no more bullshit! We have enough problems as it is."

Ragnar stooped to retrieve his mug and took a long swig of tea before he departed. "I've made a mess of things again," he admitted, and his face showed his regret. He set the empty cup down and ambled toward the manor a few paces behind his recent foe.

The other four guys went back to their table, scowling, and Bailey and Carl sat down to eat the rest of their food.

The scion shook his head. "This needs to end. If they don't catch the murderer soon, the boiling tensions here are going to rip everyone apart."

Bailey sighed. "Unfortunately, I think you're right about that."

Back in her room, Bailey found that the very idea of being commanded to just sit around, hiding and waiting for the situation to end, rankled her, but she obeyed. Fenris offered no criticism of the trainers' decisions, and once the girl had digested her breakfast, he started to run her through further instruction.

"You did well last night," he congratulated her. "It may not have felt significant, but I sensed calm and stability growing within you, a solid core that remained unaffected despite the vast flows of power between us. Possessing such a core is vital."

She bowed her head at his praise and began her next lesson.

Time passed—hours, probably, or what would have

been hours according to Earth's time. Bailey and Fenris opened another conduit, and thoughts, emotions, and interior blasts of force circulated within them both. She applied all she'd learned and maintained her composure and good judgment even as the Were-god ramped up the intensity of the arcane currents.

During a lull in the lesson, someone knocked on the door. Bailey was violently jerked out of her divine reverie by the interruption, but the core of dispassionate reason stabilized her mood almost instantly.

Fenris nodded. The girl rose to her feet, went to the door, and flung it open.

Her eyes bulged. On his knees, leaning against the doorframe, was Malkeg Ironfist. He was still armored, but someone had removed his helmet and split his head from scalp to jaw, and blood poured down his face and body. As the door moved inwards, he slumped and then toppled to the floor at her feet, dead.

Her eyes darted up and down the hall. No one was there, and she couldn't see any sign of someone having been there recently. Then again, she'd been consumed by the reverie induced by Fenris's magical seminar.

Bailey dragged the body into her room and shut the door, then looked toward the wolf-god.

He stood up, frowning deeply but oddly calm, she felt. If she had not been practicing lucidity only a moment ago, she might have panicked or rushed down the halls in a rage, seeking the killer.

Fenris shook his head. "Alas," he commented, "though it was bound to happen. The attacker, whoever he is, has taken matters into his own hands. He's removing not only his targets but those who were hunting him and protecting those targets. Leaving the body here was probably an attempt to intimidate the trainees as a whole."

Bailey struggled to find the right thing to say or do. Part of her cynically wondered if this was another test she was being put through.

To her surprise, Fenris helped her decide. He locked his dark eyes with hers.

"You have two options. Perhaps more if you consider the obviously foolish ones, but let us say two *good* options."

She was pretty sure she knew what he would say, but she listened all the same.

"First, you can remain in this room under my protection. You will be safe because if anyone moves against you, I will destroy them utterly. Everyone here is part-divine or more, and special rules govern this place, so direct intervention on my part is allowed. Frankly, I do not care about this mystery. It's a plot by another god according to their own unfathomable motivations and falls outside of my purview unless the assassin tries to harm my apprentice. Do that, and you will be secure."

She considered it. But...

"Or," Fenris went on, "you can do what I suspect you'll do anyway, which is hunt down the murderer, heedless of the rules, and protect your friends and fellow trainees." He paused. "In which case, I shall do nothing to hinder you."

The girl gave him a feral grin, one containing no humor or joy. Before the wolf-god had time to say anything more, she had stepped over the body of Malkeg, shut the door behind her, and dashed down the hallway.

She went to Carl's room first. It wasn't far from hers,

and the door was not barred. She pushed it open and found the chamber beyond empty. Frowning, she backed out and continued down the stone corridor. Everything was hushed; no one else was around.

Next she went to Ragnar's room, and it too was devoid of inhabitants. It occurred to her that her friends might have been hiding, but they were big men, and there was no place in the chambers they could have disappeared from sight unless they were using a type of magic beyond her understanding.

She completed her circuit of the manor and found nothing untoward. However, a rear door that led to the castle's inner bailey was ajar.

"I see," she murmured, then, shifting into wolf form, she bounded across the grass, returning to humanoid shape once she reached the tall and imposing stone structure.

Steps on the side of the keep led up to a simple wooden door, which she opened without needing to break it down. Beyond lay a maze of rooms and corridors similar to those in the manor-barracks but decorated more finely. No one was present here either, though she was under the impression that this was where the trainers slept and planned their moves.

Rounding a corner, she saw a flitting shadow and heard soft movement. Sucking in a breath, she dashed after the sound, which was moving ahead of her and wending its way through the halls.

Bailey ducked into a room where she'd seen a silhouette move and realized she'd trapped the fleeing person in a dead-end. The silhouette backed toward a stack of crates, and a dim shaft of torchlight fell on its face.

"Carl!" she snapped. "Why were you running away from me?"

He sighed in relief. "I didn't know it was you. Someone knocked on my door and dumped the dead body of Cerrio, one of the trainers, there for me to find. I thought I heard someone running away, so I've been stalking them."

"Shit," said Bailey. "Same thing. The bastard killed Malkeg and left him on my doorstep. I checked your and Ragnar's rooms. His was empty too. I wonder if he's out doing the same thing as us."

"Could be," the scion suggested. "Let's work together. Safety in numbers."

She agreed, and the pair turned, preparing to continue their sweep of the castle.

Ragnar stepped into the doorway.

"No," he began, cutting them off from speaking, "not the same thing as you."

Bailey noticed the strange look on the Norseman's face, a mixture of judgmental dislike, frustration, and bestial madness. Tingeing it was also the same expression he'd worn in the mess hall. Guilt.

"I was hoping I'd get you alone like this," he added. Then he attacked.

"No!" Bailey cried as the huge form of the Viking drove against them, his powerful limbs flailing like trees caught in a cyclone. Heavy blows drove them both back in different directions. Ragnar roared like an enraged bear, blocking Bailey with a simple magical shield, then turning his aggression on Carl.

For all that he was formidable, Carl was disoriented by the initial strike. Ragnar plowed into him unchallenged, the huge fists ramming into the scion's ribs and face. Bailey regained control of herself and hurled a static electrical net at Ragnar as Carl tried to push the Norseman away from him with a magically-augmented kick.

Ragnar shrugged off their magic. He let out awful snarling and groaning sounds, his eyes gleamed with insanity. Foamy spittle had formed around his mouth. Bailey didn't know what was going on, but she had an idea.

The berserkers, the dreaded and bloodthirsty shock-troops of the ancient Norse, capable of entering an altered state of consciousness where they killed and destroyed indiscriminately and were impervious to most harm. Ragnar was one of them, and he had the power of divine blood behind him to boot.

Bailey pounced at him, conjuring a long red plasma lance from her fist, but he knocked her aside with shocking speed before the blade could do any more than graze him. She collapsed into a mass of crates, shattering them, while Ragnar shook Carl and pummeled him nearly into uncon-sciousness.

Summoning her full power, Bailey blasted the Viking warrior with a relentless whirlwind that lifted him off his feet and pinned him against the wall. While he struggled against it, she grabbed Carl and pulled him to safety.

Ragnar somehow broke free after only a second or two, and he dashed back to the doorway, cutting them off.

The werewitch stared at him. "What's the matter with you? We were friends, goddammit!"

For an instant, it seemed he would answer her question, and his face looked almost human. Then the bestial crazi-ness returned, and he howled, "I can't live without it.

Blood! Battle! It's *who I am*. Don't you understand? Freya promised me all I could handle. So much!"

He laughed, and there was a nauseating note of despair in the sound. She imagined him as a druggie who had abandoned himself to his addiction.

"Freya?" Bailey asked. Carl, clinging to her shoulder, found his feet and struggled to stand up straight.

Ragnar chuckled again, nastily but with restraint. The terrifying light in his eyes had not diminished, though. "She dispatched me to keep an eye on you and destroy anyone I deemed a threat. But who *isn't* a threat? *All* of them were! There's no way to know when friends will become enemies. Betrayal, war, and murder are the ways of the world. That's what I live for. I have to! I need it!"

Carl muttered, "We found the murderer. Too bad he's also a scion."

"Dammit," Bailey snapped, not wanting to believe this was happening. Not wanting to lose another friend. "We weren't going to betray you, Ragnar. No one else was, either. Stop this right now. We can work something out."

"No," Ragnar rumbled. "Freya *wants* you dead. She won't admit it, but she fears you coming for her throne as the goddess of sorcery. She dislikes your involvement with Fenris, whom she fears above all others. You seem..." he swallowed, "nice, but you must die. My lady demands it, and she will reward me with an eternity of red, raging strife. Never-ending violence!"

Grasping that Ragnar was a lost cause, that the undertow of insanity within him was stronger than any part of him that was decent and human, Bailey threw another cyclone, combined with every other offensive magic she could think of. The doorframe broke apart around the berserker, and the walls started to melt.

Ragnar stood amidst it, shielding his face but taking no great damage. Then he plunged toward her, his teeth bared.

CHAPTER NINE

Agent Velasquez and Agent Park sat on a bench on a pleasant and peaceful street in West Seattle, dressed in their dark suits (which weren't *quite* black, more of a deep greenish-gray) and dark glasses, eating the hoagies they'd picked up at a local sandwich shop.

And that was all. They did nothing else. There was nothing else *to* do.

Life is good, Velasquez thought. *I'll make it home in one piece, and I should have time to get a high-quality workout in AND watch Netflix for a couple hours.*

He had had to admit, the good life could be rather dull.

Park was taking the situation less well.

"You know," the man grated, and it seemed that his scalp reddened beneath his buzzcut, "as happy as I am not to die and to see that things in Seattle are nice and cozy and shit, I was under the impression that the taxpayer dollars that pay my salary would be going toward doing something other than playing handheld games and sampling the goddamn local cuisine."

Velasquez chortled. "You tell 'em, Park. Good job. We need agents like you on the force."

His junior partner had to laugh at that, but his look of irritation gradually returned. "I mean, what about the Venatori? Shouldn't someone be keeping an eye on them?"

The senior agent shook his head. "Negative. We can keep an eye on them from home, and our jurisdiction is strictly within the United States. We're like the supernatural version of the FBI. I'm pretty sure overseas supernatural shit is handled by the same people who handle the non-supernatural shit, so if you want to join the CIA for whatever reason, there's that."

Park shuddered. "I have *some* standards," he grumbled.

Having finished his hoagie, Velasquez crumpled up the wrapping paper and tossed it into a nearby garbage can. Then he leaned back and allowed the warm sunshine to fall on his face.

He sighed. "I'll confess that things have been borderline pointless lately without Hurricane Bailey and her entourage of natural disasters fucking everything up. It's like that Broken Window Fallacy or whatever they call it, where someone has to break something so someone else can have a job cleaning it up. We're the cleaners."

Park nodded. "Good. Next time someone walks their dog and doesn't take care of the mess, I'll be right there with a pooper-scooper."

Velasquez reached into his pocket. His mobile device had buzzed him, which could mean any of several things. When he checked it, he saw that it was the program that pinged nearby paranormals and warned him if they gathered in significant numbers, if groups of them moved toward each other, or if there were any signs of large magical expenditures.

"Well, well, well," he remarked as he opened the program to view the details. "We might get some action after all."

Park tensed with excitement and leaned over to look at Velasquez's phone.

The app showed two groups approaching the intersection about three hundred yards from the bench. One was a cluster of five or six were-shifters coming from the south, the other a quartet of witches from the north.

Trying not to salivate, the junior agent asked, "Are they gonna fight?"

"Hmm." Velasquez looked up. The two groups had come into visual range now. He motioned for Park to follow him and they strolled casually toward the lycanthropes, who waited to cross the street to the north. The witches on the other side of the road appeared to be waiting for them.

When the crosswalk permitted them to go, the Weres moved out. The two agents remained where they were, pretending to be absorbed in checking something on their phones.

Behind him, Velasquez heard most of the conversation between the two groups as they met.

"Hey, you made it," a gruff voice quipped. "Probably helps that it's a sunny day for once."

A woman laughed and replied, "I hate the sun. It ruins my goddamn complexion."

"Yeah," someone added, "like pizza grease is any better."

"I thought we were going out for sushi?"

A Were grunted. "Why not both?"

They set off northward together, chatting and seeking lunch.

Park kicked the nearest lamppost. "For fuck's sake. There's so much harmony and crap that we don't even get to break up street brawls. I should have joined the regular-ass *cops*."

"That would have been something," Velasquez mused. "I don't see a lot of Korean cops."

Park snorted. "You're not originally from Southern California, are you?"

"Nope. Pacific Northwest born and bred," the senior agent replied. "Wanna wander south and see if any vampires are up early?"

Having nothing better to do, they made for a nightclub Velasquez had heard of with blacked-out windows.

Halfway there, though, the senior agent got a call. He pulled out his phone, glanced at the screen, and was surprised to see that it was Headquarters.

He swiped the green icon. "Velasquez."

"You've got a case, agent," said the voice on the other end. "Urgent, Class Two. Report to Rendezvous Point Six-C at once. Over and out."

Park smiled. "I heard that."

"I'm sure you did." Velasquez opened the remote key app he used to summon their car and punched in the necessary information, then stood and waited. Park seemed far less antsy now that there was a guarantee of something interesting going on.

Three minutes later, a long black Maybach, complete with blue HID lights, pulled up at the curb, seemingly of its own accord. A handful of passersby and loiterers took notice of the vehicle as the two agents stepped toward it.

Agent Velasquez had taken particular pleasure in seizing this vehicle, which one of the Venatori's sycophants had driven in the US, and had tagged it for his own use without much demur from on high, having it refitted with lights and the other bells and whistles required during execution of his job.

The doors opened with the distinctive hissing sound that had always reminded Velasquez of Darth Vader breathing through his helmet. Then the men in suits and sunglasses climbed into the car, which set off through the streets, leaving behind pedestrians who stared after it with slack jaws.

The door to the castle storeroom widened to something like the ragged mouth of a cavern as the supporting beams and stones burned and melted. Debris flew and floated on swirling winds and powerful electromagnetic currents. The ceiling was starting to buckle and looked like it might collapse.

Bailey grunted, straining as the full strength of her abilities fought the magically empowered wrath of the berserker. Despite his apparent lack of self-control, Ragnar was winning. His raw power, experience, and madness were too much.

Carl was back in the fight, though. He assailed Ragnar from the sides and rear with small blasts of magic as well as psionic confusion spells. Though he was still recovering from his severe beating, his contribution was enough to distract the Norseman from maintaining his shield.

A mass of arcane fury swept over Ragnar and drove him back, stumbling and then rolling through the hall, his clothes smoking. Bailey pulled Carl out through the ravaged door, and they started down a perpendicular corridor. Bailey conjured a quick shield behind them.

They'd made it halfway when Ragnar came around the corner, bellowing like an enraged animal and hurling magic with wild abandon. A blast struck the pair from behind and exploded the magical barrier, and they tumbled forward.

Bailey jumped back to her feet, not badly affected. It looked like Carl was struggling not to pass out, though. She took his arm.

"Go on," she told him, "get help. I can hold him off until you come back with the cavalry."

He shook his head sharply as Ragnar laughed behind them, pausing to savor his next attack.

"I can't," Carl protested. "I'll stay with you. I've been ordered to."

"What?" Bailey's stomach clenched. "Don't tell me..." Her voice trailed off as Ragnar stomped closer, and she spun to face him.

Standing by her side, Carl elaborated. "Ragnar's not the only agent here. Balder sent me. I'm one of his apprentices, here on his behalf to observe and aid. Just like our friend there." He gestured at the berserker. "I, however, *don't* feel that you're a threat and decided the best thing I could do was aid you."

The Norseman had stopped, staring at them and grinning in his insane way, exerting the minimum of self-control necessary to stretch out the moment before he moved in for the kill. And, it seemed, he was giving Carl time to finish speaking.

The dark-skinned scion went on, "I know I'm not part of the Norse pantheon, and it's not something I'd thought about before. My mother was a goddess from a completely different tradition, but Balder took me under his wing anyway. He found me at a low ebb in my life, felt bad for me, and chose to train me in magic and combat. I owe him everything."

Bailey was not offended. Carl might have been standing with her because it was his job, but he was still a friend as far as she was concerned. "Let's do this together, then. Balder's boy and Fenris' girl against Freya's rabid dog."

Hearing her put it that way, a strange abashed look came over Ragnar's face. Rage replaced it again, but now it was bitter and frustrated anger rather than ravenous bloodthirst. The Viking turned and ran.

"What the…" Carl stammered.

Bailey sputtered, "He might kill someone else. C'mon, after him!"

The two broke into a sprint at the same instant, taking long strides around the corner and down the hall. They saw with sinking hearts that Ragnar was faster than they were, despite running at top speed. The obscure forces that gave him his strength, speed, and endurance were beyond anything Bailey knew how to counter.

As the berserker passed out of sight, thumps and screams and crashes resounded through the castle. Bailey didn't know how many inhabited the structure; she could only conclude that Ragnar, in a desperate effort to sow as much chaos as he could and pin some of it on Bailey, had abandoned all restraint and was killing and destroying everyone and everything he came across.

"I can't do this," the girl gasped, "not in this form."

She let herself fall forward, and when she struck the floor, she stood on four legs.

"Bailey!" Carl shouted from behind her as she outpaced him. She knew he'd catch up quickly, but first, *she* needed to catch up with Ragnar.

They came to a staircase, and the Norseman came into sight. His blind rage was so severe by this point that the minor obstacle of steps had distracted him. He'd paused to kick the steps, breaking some off and sending chunks of stone in all directions.

In wolf form, Bailey bounded upward and seized Ragnar by the ankle with her jaws. He was too big, strong, and heavy for her to trip, but she threw him off-balance. Before he could recover, she shifted back into humanoid form, kicked him in the groin, and punched him in the face.

He fell back a step or two, but despite her strength, she'd done little more than stun and annoy him. His mouth foamed and his big, hammer-like hands latched onto her waist and shoulder, and he picked her up like a limp mannequin and slammed her into the wall hard enough to crack it.

Pain exploded through her body and dimmed her consciousness. Gritting her teeth, she forced herself to roll aside, barely missing the blow from Ragnar's fist where her face had been. His knee and shin took her in the back of the legs, and she tumbled down the steps.

Carl passed her as she fell. Both scions stood at the top of the staircase, half-crouched in fighting stances, and began to circle one another.

Bailey sprang to her feet. She held her head between both hands to steady her vision, and she heard the two speaking to each other over the pounding of blood through her skull.

"You're dead," Ragnar snarled. "Neither of you can match my strength."

"I'm the child of a shapeshifter as well as a goddess," Carl threw back. "Which means, yes, I can."

His form distorted and grew bigger, taking on the exact dimensions of his opponent. The werewitch hoped the transformation would also grant him the berserker's incredible physical power.

Bailey started rushing back up the steps as the two hulking figures crashed into each other. Their impact resembled a none-too-distant thunderclap and sent a tremor through the stone castle. Bailey had to steady herself. Dust fell from the ceiling.

Wavering snarls and howls of bestial fury erupted from the struggling pair. They smote each other's faces and chests with blows that would have put holes in a solid concrete wall, grappling with enough force to uproot mature oak trees. They spat rippling explosions of magic as soon as they had the elbow room.

The girl shielded herself from the worst fallout of the struggle, then dove toward Ragnar's right leg, punching and kicking his knee.

Carl shouted, "Get back!"

Ragnar's thick arm swept toward Bailey's face, but she was pirouetting back and away from it. Carl piled into the berserker.

I can't go toe to toe with him. With either of them, she concluded. *Only magic will work at this point.*

As Carl forced Ragnar away from her, moving the battle down the second-floor hall, Bailey listened carefully, then reached out with her arcane consciousness and felt for the stomping feet of the two combatants. Once she had a firm bead on the Norseman, she cast the spell.

The stone beneath his feet melted into a small pit of lava that was knee-deep. He roared in pain and shock; his divine resistance was strong enough that he didn't burst into flames or melt, but it clearly was hurting him, and it gave Carl the opportunity to land a full-force blow on the side of his head.

The punch hit harder than Bailey could have imagined. She heard bone crunch, and the berserker's head spun and wobbled in ways that looked unnatural as his entire body rose into the air from the lava hole and flopped on the floor, his legs smoking.

He didn't rise again. Bailey ran to his side as Carl crouched, ready to fight more if need be.

Ragnar was still alive, but he was severely wounded. His neck was broken, and a section of his skull had cracked inward. He coughed up blood.

"Bailey...Carl," he gasped. "You would have made...fine friends."

Carl's form altered subtly as he returned to his usual shape, which was imposing but not as massive as Ragnar's.

The Viking warrior turned his gaze to the face of Bailey, who stood watching him and biting her lip.

"Forgive me," he pleaded. His voice had fallen to a whisper. "The old call...to violence and battle... If not for it...we might have been..."

His voice trailed off, and his body stiffened while his eyes went glassy. Bailey put a hand over her face and shook her head.

Carl, breathing heavily, came to her side and put his hand on her arm. "We need to go tell the other trainers what happened. There might be other people who were wounded who need help."

"Yeah," Bailey agreed. They hurried back down the stairs. "More people who might have been friends if things were different."

<hr>

All courses and activities had been suspended until further notice. With two of the trainers and several members of the support staff dead, the damage done to the keep, and a general atmosphere of dread, anger, and sadness suffusing the grounds, it was agreed that everyone needed time to recover.

The students had all been sent to their rooms while the surviving staff dealt with the mess. Bailey had hugged Carl before dropping him off at his room. Then she'd returned to her own to reconvene with Fenris.

"*This*," the wolf-god boomed, "is outrageous. I cannot *believe* her! What was she *thinking?*" His fist shot out and turned a chair into a shower of splinters, which he kicked into the roaring fireplace.

Bailey watched, stunned. She had never seen her mentor like this. The only time he'd come close to this level of unrestrained fury was when a group of wolves from the Eastmoor pack had tried to deny her right to ascend to High Shaman. He'd killed one of them, revealing his true form in the process, to obtain their obedience to his will.

He'd still been in control of himself then. Now, Fenris seemed to be barely containing the same type of rage Ragnar had fed upon during his crazed rampage.

The deity ranted, "Freya was completely reckless to do this. Sloppy, careless, and frankly, stupid. Her presumptuousness and paranoia went too far this time. She might not have given Ragnar the order to murder all those students and make an attempt on your life, but it matters not. What did she expect to happen? She chose a berserker, one who was downright unstable and disturbed and permitted him to use his own judgment to decide whether and who to kill. She *must* have known this would happen! Damn her!"

In a sheepish voice, Bailey added, "It makes even less sense when you consider that Carl was sent by Balder. I thought Balder and Freya were on the same team? What the hell happened?"

"She's unfit," Fenris snapped. "I'm tempted to challenge her myself, but I cannot. If I did, it would bring down ruin upon too much of the universe. At the very least, she ought to be removed temporarily if not permanently from the council and forbidden any greater leadership position than presiding over benign witches. Clearly she has lost her right to dictate what happens in the world of rising demigods."

Bailey sat down and poured herself a glass of water. It was barely suppertime, but she felt like she was ready to pass out for the night. "Shit," she muttered, unable to think of anything clever or useful to say.

Fenris's nostrils flared as he breathed in, then let it out slowly. He regained his composure and eased back into his usual stoic demeanor.

"I am sorry for coming so close to losing control like that," he told the Were. "But I'm stunned at what my sister allowed to happen. I can't retaliate against her for this, but you can."

Bailey arched her eyebrows, terrified that he meant...

"No," the wolf-father said, holding up a hand palm outward as though reading her thoughts. "I don't mean for you to kill her as you did Aradia. The necessary solution is subtler and gentler, along the lines of what I said a moment ago about removing her from the council until she sees reason."

"You mean," Bailey surmised, "present a case that Freya screwed this up badly enough for the other gods to kick her out? Something like that?"

"Essentially, yes," he confirmed. "But not yet. We should strengthen our own position before we move."

The werewitch had four or five different ideas about what that might mean, and none sounded any more likely than the others. "How so?"

Fenris clasped his hands behind his back, and he slowly began pacing around the room. "It would involve remaining here for a while. Continuing your training.

Continuing the process of meeting people—gods-to-be, future champions of the various divine pantheons—and winning them over, getting their trust and support. Do you think you could do that?"

Bailey hesitated. She was fairly confident that she could, but it seemed odd to her. After what had happened with the murders, the training ground might not function properly for a time.

And, her mind added, *how does making more friends help me boot Freya off the council? I don't understand.*

Rather than pressing her for a response, Fenris continued, "What I intend, you see, is for you to build a base of supporters. People who will vouch for you, and furthermore, who some of the other gods will listen to. If enough beings join you and confirm your integrity, the conclave will have little choice but to pay attention when you explain to them how Freya jeopardized everyone with her little scheme."

It was a minute or so before Bailey replied.

"I'm not so sure," she began. "It seems…I dunno, weird to me. What happened was a big enough deal that I would have thought we should do something about it right away. But then again, I don't understand the way things work between the gods yet. You'd know better than I would, and I've always had good reason to trust your judgment."

"Good." Fenris thanked her with a solemn nod. "As for the immediate present, I'm sure you're tired, but if you can manage, I would like to further your training while I'm able."

She cracked her neck and drew in a breath. "I think I

can do that. I've been through worse. More of the stuff from last night?"

"Not quite," he elaborated. "What we learned last night will help you overall, but tonight I think we should focus on the specifics of combat. In particular, defense. You haven't had to confront many if any beings who are equal to or greater than you in terms of raw magical power. Your skill with the use of shields has improved, but there are other things you can do to protect yourself from being overwhelmed by strong opponents."

"Oh?" she asked, curious. "Might help, I'll admit."

The wolf-god came closer to her. "Yes. Ways of using shields you haven't thought of yet. Ways of maximizing their deflection potential. Also wards, which you don't seem to know anything about. A ward is a kind of 'smart shield,' you might say, which can be activated and then left to operate on its own, though it will only protect you from certain types of attacks. Still, it means not having to concentrate on maintaining a conventional shield all the time."

Bailey blinked. "Damn. Wish I'd known about those earlier."

Offering no feedback on her last comment, Fenris raised his arms and began his lesson.

Bailey listened, rapt and appreciative, as her teacher explained how to identify different types of magic, elemental and otherwise, in the atmosphere around her or in the basic composition of reality. These magics, if present even in infinitesimal quantities, could be used much like antiviruses to create arcane locus points that would negate any magic involving the same elements, and the wards would follow her around for a fair amount of time—as long as an hour if properly constructed—and offer ongoing protection.

"Let us begin," Fenris extrapolated, "with heat. We have a fireplace in this room, and fire is traditionally one of the first elements any student learns to manipulate. Begin by thinking about the heat in the room and identifying how it is woven into the fabric of all that surrounds us."

In a way, Bailey philosophized, *it's like starting over from scratch and being a newbie again, but I know enough that learning to make wards should take a lot less time than all the other shit did.*

As the night progressed, she learned that she was correct.

CHAPTER TEN

The werewitch opened her eyes.

At the end of the evening, her lesson in warding and advanced shielding completed, she'd fallen into a deep slumber that had seemingly commenced within three heartbeats of her head striking the pillow. She didn't know how long she'd slept, but it felt like an entire day.

She sat up. "Fenris. How long was I out?"

The tall man was seated at their table, perusing an old leather-bound book. He snapped it shut with one hand. "Long enough. It is now late morning by the time kept in this realm. They'll shut down the mess hall soon, so I will fetch your breakfast myself while you stretch your legs and wash your face."

She thanked him and he departed, then she began her brief start-of-the-day preparations.

As Bailey freshened up, she reflected on last night's endeavors. It hadn't taken long for her to get the hang of a basic and functional anti-heat ward. It was somewhat sloppy and would have lasted for less time than would be ideal, but it had served its purpose. She'd been able to stick her hands into the fire without needing to shield herself and come out unharmed.

Her mentor had also explained the idea behind full deflective shields, how they had to be made of arcane matter that had a curved surface and a "springy" or grease-like structure, the better to send an opponent's attacks back at them. They'd run out of time and energy before they could attempt to conjure one.

Fenris returned carrying a tray piled with a platter of steaming egg and sausage scramble, a hunk of cheese, a thick slice of toasted bread, and a mug of honeyed tea. He set it down in front of her on the table, and she thanked him before she dug in.

"Did you eat?" she asked him around a mouthful of toast and eggs.

"No," he answered her, "but I am not hungry. I hunted when we got here. Only in the mortal world do I find myself wanting to eat often."

She shrugged. "Yeah, fair enough."

The lupine deity seemed distant while Bailey completed her meal, as though he were thinking about something that had little to do with her. She asked him what was on his mind.

"My family," he responded. He continued to stare into space.

She slurped the last of her tea. "Gotcha. Families are pretty complicated, aren't they? Mine's not too bad. I imagine yours has a few more problems. Wanna tell me about it? I've always been curious about this stuff."

He made a low sound in his throat, then inclined his

head. "I suppose it would not hurt to tell you the whole story. It might be useful to know since you will essentially be joining the pantheon soon."

"Exactly," she confirmed and leaned back in her chair, folding her hands behind her head as her stomach set to work on digesting the huge breakfast she'd massacred.

Fenris put his big hands on the table before him, then looked at the girl as he began.

"It all goes back to the war between the Æsir and the Vanir, two groups of gods and immortal beings who were originally antithetical to one another but eventually blended and mingled. The Vanir preside over the domains of earth, fertility, wisdom, and soothsaying, including much of what we now know as sorcery. The Æsir represent battle, courage, truth, and justice, which are the values humanity most commonly associates with us. Long ago, before my birth, the two groups clashed during the dark primeval era, when battles between the deities ravaged all planes of existence."

Bailey focused intently on the wolf-father's words. She hadn't heard of the conflict he described. She knew only a smattering of the most basic stories from Norse mythology since Were culture paid little attention to anyone besides Fenris.

"The Æsir are generally considered to have won, though narrowly. It was a Pyrrhic victory, and the terms set at the end of hostilities represented a truce more than a conquest. The two groups began to parse out their mutual dominion. Tensions remain, but the days of open war are long past. Odin, the chief of our pantheon, is of the Æsir, and so are his children Thor and Balder. Freya, Loki, and I are of the Vanir."

The werewitch furrowed her brow. "I thought you were all brothers and sisters," she commented.

The wolf-father waved a hand in a vague gesture. "In a manner of speaking, yes. It is complicated. Our families are not like those of mortals. Except, of course," he added with a small, rueful smile, "in that parents and children still disagree, and siblings tease and pressure and occasionally resent one another, and there are many invisible dynamics that make no sense to an outside observer."

Bailey chuckled at that, though she knew that it was a dark joke. She got along well with her family, but the Nordins had their secret inner workings, as did anyone else. She knew of families that were far more dysfunctional, though.

Fenris went on, "I was an accident of sorts, a bastard child born to my father Loki and the giantess Angrbodha. Some feel I do not qualify as a full god. Some think that my parentage, being part *jotun*, makes me dangerous, so I've always been the black sheep. It is this lingering prejudice on the council's part that keeps me from sitting in any of their chairs."

Hearing that, Bailey's heart ached, and she reached out to put a hand atop those of her mentor. Her immediate family had always accepted her, but until recently, her wider family—her pack—had not.

Fenris continued, "It has been ages upon ages, with me trying my best to minister to my people, the Weres, though I am not given the full complement of dignity usually afforded a god."

Bailey assured him, "It's okay. I understand in a lot of ways, believe me. I think I went through the mortal version of the same thing."

"I suppose you did," he acknowledged. He went on to describe the details of the internal politics of both his brood within the Norse pantheon and the council, which included deities from other traditions. He told her of uncertain ties, of vague yet all-encompassing expectations, of confused emotions and lingering resentments that had played out across millennia as entire human civilizations rose and fell.

"So," he wrapped up, "you can see part of the reason I chose you to be my protege, beyond your obvious power and talent. Your situation, in a fashion, mirrored my own. For all that your position in shifter society was that of a virtual outcast, you have since become a hero and your people's champion."

She grinned. "Thanks. I try not to let it go to my head, but not gonna lie, it's nice hearing you put it like that."

"Of course." He returned the smile, but it faded quickly back to his usual stony expression. "But your rise has led us directly to our current predicament. You have, without intending to, upset the other gods and goddesses. You've forced them to alter their thinking about mortals and the types of possibilities that they allow for them. That is significant, Bailey. And though they feel you've been a force of chaos, you have also been a force for unity between Weres and witches, something never seen before.

"The script has changed. They recognize possibilities for good in what you've done, but they also feel threatened by it. You can see how immortal beings who have existed for eons would be frightened by things that are new and different."

Bailey thought back to conversations she'd had with Roland about how they both sometimes felt as though hollow, hidebound traditions were holding them back. "It makes sense," she agreed. "It's like when all those alphas and shamans thought I was coming to take away their positions, though that wasn't the idea."

"Of course." Fenris's mood darkened in an odd way. "Given what happened yesterday, it seems fair to say that one deity in particular is more threatened by you than any other."

She frowned. "Yeah, I guess."

The wolf-father stood up. "I do not mean to imply that my sister is...evil, only that she's been compromised by her feelings and overreactions to recent events. Freya's mindset is irrational, and if it does not improve, things will get worse for us."

"So," Bailey queried, "how do we improve it?"

"Any way we can. But," Fenris added, "it may not be possible. We can try to persuade her with both words and deeds, but we cannot change her fundamental nature. If she refuses to see reason, there is the possibility of...confrontation."

The girl didn't like the sound of that.

"You told me before you didn't expect us to fight. I sure as hell don't want to, and it wasn't that long ago that the two of you made a truce and helped me revive Roland. It's not like she's anywhere near as bad as Aradia, right?" She stared into the darkness under his hood.

He spread his hands and shook his head. "I do not

know. We will try everything else first, but we must consider that it *might* happen. If it does, you must be ready. I think we should run through a basic review of how to fight a goddess, and how, if need be, to kill one."

I did that once, Bailey thought. *No desire to do it again, but Fenris is probably right. It's better to be safe than sorry, and he knows Freya a lot better than I do.*

"Consider," her mentor extrapolated, "all the deaths she's indirectly responsible for through her choice of Ragnar to watch over you. Consider also how many people back home you're responsible for now. If Freya decides that you are her potential enemy, all those people could be in danger."

The girl put her hands over her face and shook her head. "I don't want it to come to that. We just finished one war against a goddess, and we don't need another one. Shit!" She sighed. "Let's do the review, then, but let's also talk to her *before* we try anything more drastic, y'know?"

Fenris stared at her. "So be it." He motioned for her to rise. She got up, then strode across the floor to the open space before the fireplace.

"*If,*" the wolf-father began, "you must fight the Lady of Sorcery, then there are two things to remember, both of which are of immense importance. The first is that the basic process is no different from when you battled Aradia—grounding yourself, opening up a conduit between you and her, and draining her power. The second is that Freya is substantially stronger than Aradia was, so you would not be able to overpower her through brute force. You'd have to fight defensively, relying on your Were abilities to give you the physical strength to resist the process rather than meeting her on even ground in a duel of magic."

She frowned. "I see."

Fenris rubbed his chin. "I'd like you to practice once again, using me as an anchor and reservoir. Oh, and a final thing to consider. It might come to pass that you must fight Freya without killing her. Embarrassing her could compromise her position and force her off the council. Then she would be bereft of the clout that led to yesterday's disaster."

Bailey hadn't thought about it that way. "Okay. Let's get started."

Someone knocked on the door. After their long discussion and practice regimen, Bailey and Fenris had relaxed, taking a break before they resumed the werewitch's defensive magical training.

The werewitch stood up. "I'll get it." She left Fenris sitting by the fire, though he kept an eye on her in case a new threat emerged.

Beyond the door stood Carl. "Hello," he greeted her. "Am I disturbing you? If not, I'd like to talk for a few minutes."

"Nah," Bailey informed him. "We were chilling out before we worked on some stuff. Come in."

The scion stepped over the threshold and immediately locked eyes with her mentor.

"Hello," he said again. "I don't believe we've met."

Bailey and the wolf-god exchanged a quick glance, and

she sensed that it would be better not to divulge his true identity. She recalled the name her teacher had gone by when he'd posed as a mortal.

"This is Marcus," she explained. "He's a veteran were-shaman from the Cascade Mountains back on Earth. He's been by my side this whole time, teaching me new stuff every step of the way. I would never have gotten this far without him."

Fenris rose and shook the other man's hand. "Good to meet you. Bailey seems to like and trust you."

Carl squirmed a tad at the comment as though it embarrassed him. "Well, that's good to know. Anyhow, at this point, the proverbial cat is out of the bag. As I said before, yes, I was sent by Balder to watch you, Bailey. I hope you still trust me, regardless. There was no facade, nothing dishonest about how hard I fought Ragnar. It was to protect everyone, but you especially. I don't think you're a threat to the council or anyone else unless they deserve it. I mean no harm. Nothing I've seen inclines me to deliver a negative report to my patron. Ragnar only thought you were dangerous because he was crazy. I wanted to clear the air between us."

The girl watched his face as he spoke. It occurred to her that a shapeshifter would make an excellent liar, but somehow she didn't think he was trying to deceive her. And it was true about the recent fight with the berserker; he'd saved her life.

"Okay," she remarked. "You're forgiven, and I see no reason for us to stop being friends. I'm glad I know the truth, but I believe you. Balder never seemed like he bore me any ill will. He confronted my boyfriend and me once and tested us, but he just seemed, I dunno, cautious. Not hostile."

Both Fenris and Carl nodded. "Yes," affirmed the scion, "that sounds exactly like him."

They chatted about other things then, obliquely discussing the techniques they'd used in their fight with Ragnar without having to discuss the Viking since deep down, they both regretted having to kill him. Bailey revealed more about her background, though she took care not to divulge who Fenris was while she was at it.

After a short while, the shaman entered the conversation. "Carl," he began, "I am curious to see you in action. The particular combination of heritages you represent is uncommon, so I'd like to know what you can do."

Carl smiled but fidgeted, obviously feeling like he'd been put on the spot. "Well, what would you like to see?" he asked.

A sly twist found its way to Fenris's mouth. "How well you fight," he said. "I'm curious what skills Balder imbues his students with. Not against me, though, against an individual at your level. Bailey, for example."

The girl cocked an eyebrow at her teacher before looking at Carl. He seemed uncertain, but she told him, "Might be a good training exercise. Are we allowed, though? I dunno why they're keeping us in our damn rooms since the threat has been neutralized."

Fenris moved toward the door. "I'll take care of it. Come. I think we all would do well to get some fresh air right now."

The werewitch and the scion followed. Bailey put a hand on Carl's arm.

"Don't worry," she reassured him, "Marcus is a hell of a teacher. He can be rough, but he wouldn't want anything bad to happen to either of us. Besides, this oughta be fun."

He shrugged his broad shoulders. "I suppose so."

They closed the door behind them and traversed the halls toward the main entrance to the manor-barracks, where a pair of valets tried to stop them.

Fenris drew himself up to his full height. "Let us pass," he demanded, his voice low but powerful. "You know who I am. It would be better for everyone if you did not interfere with my wishes. The murderer has been dealt with, and I'll not have my pupil's time wasted. She and her sparring partner need training as long as they're here. I shall supervise."

One of the valets bit his lip. The other hemmed and hawed and tried to resist, but he soon gave up and allowed the trio to leave the building.

Fenris took them out and then through the inner gates toward a dirt yard behind the keep they hadn't seen, which was enclosed by a low circular wall. It reminded Bailey of a small, crude gladiatorial arena.

The god pointed at a nearby outbuilding. "That is where the trainers store all the weapons and armor they brought out for you to choose from during the melee. Help yourselves."

Bailey and Carl went into the small warehouse, where they saw the familiar lineup of dummies outfitted in armor, along with racks and racks of armaments.

The scion laughed. "I could stand to blow off some steam. The tension from that lockdown combined with having to sit in our rooms most of the time is driving me insane."

"Same," Bailey agreed. "I'll say in advance, though, that it's nothing personal when I kick your ass."

"Likewise." He saluted her and dug into the buffet of accessories.

Both trainees selected the outfits they'd worn during the free-for-all, with Bailey making sure to don the cape with its magic-reflecting scales. She traded in her second short sword for a light warhammer, figuring it would allow her to inflict more impact damage on Carl's heavier armor. He, meanwhile, chose the same heavy one-handed mace and powerful gauntlet he'd used previously.

They emerged and passed through the simple gate in the round wall. Fenris was standing atop one of the thick posts, and he watched them as they padded to the dusty ground in the center of the arena.

The shaman raised his hands. "Rules. Do not kill one another, and you may use magic, which you will find works normally here, as it did during your spat with Ragnar. In fact, I encourage you," he paused, "to employ what you've learned in your most recent lessons."

Ah, I get it, Bailey concluded, *Carl's part-god, so he wants me to practice what I'd need to do to fight Freya.*

"Begin," Fenris said.

Carl charged, and Bailey swept to the side before he'd completed his first step. The scion whirled and lashed out with his mace, conjuring a wall of fire three or four steps behind the girl's position to keep her from retreating too far out of his threat range.

She retaliated by sending a thin bolt of kinetic force

toward his legs, knocking him to his knees, then charging in, whirling her weapons. He blocked her hammer with his mace and deflected the weaker blow of her sword with his armored fist.

They separated, circling each other. Bailey thought since they both were armored that Carl might try electrocuting her. She focused on the subtle threads of electromagnetic energy in the air around them and constructed a quick and cheap but serviceable ward against lightning spells that appeared briefly as a whitish glyph floating in the air over her shoulder and then went invisible. She could feel its lingering protection.

Carl instantly tossed a thunderbolt. She wondered if he knew what she'd done and was testing to confirm it. The deadly electrical surge fizzled uselessly about two feet from her face.

"Ha!" She sneered. "Nice try." Then they clashed, and her world became a whirlwind of sweat and clanging steel.

Bailey rapidly found herself on the defensive. Though not as massive as Ragnar, Carl approached him in terms of being a physical powerhouse. He had more reach and upper-body muscle mass than she did, and his divine heritage made him a match for her extra strength as a lycanthrope. She fell back from the onslaught of his heavy blows, grasping that she'd need to try different tactics.

She sprang away, dodging nimbly and forcing him to chase her. He did at first, then switched to unleashing blasts of magic, including the occasional lightning bolt that continued to be absorbed by her electrical ward.

Bailey concentrated, her mind seeking the godly part of her opponent. During his next attack, a whirling projectile of sonic vibrations and ice-cold wind, she *felt* the source of his power, just as she felt Fenris nearby. He would be an anchor if she needed one.

The girl caught the whirlwind of sound and cold and tossed it aside, then envisioned a pronged wire emerging from her chest to plug into Carl's heart. She secured it to the ground and felt his power seeping out.

He gasped and tossed a hasty fireball at her, and she used her cloak's scales to deflect it, thinking the structure of the cloak was much like the structure of the shields Fenris had told her about last night.

Sensing that his magic had weakened, Carl resumed attacking using brute force. Any of his furious blows might have knocked her out, and he was pretty fast. Bailey was faster, and her shifter capabilities and long training with Fenris had given her stamina and endurance he couldn't match.

He began to falter. Exulting in the prospect of victory, Bailey struck him with a wave of gently-electrified water that paralyzed him with nasty static shocks, then hit him with a blast of cold, freezing the moisture that had gotten through the cracks in his armor. He could barely move. She jump-kicked him to the ground, then whacked his breastplate with her hammer and his helmet with her sword.

Carl reeled but swiped up with his mace while grabbing her ankle with his gauntleted left hand. There was no way to dodge the blow entirely. Instead, she turned her body so it glanced off her chest, conjuring a spring and a rippling shield at the point of impact.

Her hasty magic wasn't perfect, but it was enough that

the mace struck with only about a quarter of the force it should have had. She let out an *oof,* but she wasn't injured. She hit Carl with another electrical shock, followed by a second strike to his helmet with her hammer. Her ward protected her from being shocked as the metal head of the bludgeon struck the sparking steel.

Carl raised a hand. "Yield," he gasped.

Bailey stepped back, breathing heavily. "Not bad," she congratulated him. Out of the corner of her eye, she saw Fenris watching her closely and listening.

The scion had trouble getting up after the drubbing he'd taken, so she helped him to his feet and shook his hand. "It was a good fight," she said. "You're damn strong and fast. I guess I'm used to having to fight many different kinds of opponents creatively."

He shook his head and pulled off his dented helmet. "Did you do something to me? I suddenly felt...drained, and my magic wasn't working as well as it should have."

"Not that I can recall," she lied, sensing that she ought not reveal what Fenris had taught her to do. "I threw a lot of shit at you, and it all happened too fast to think about it too hard. In all fairness, I barely won."

The tall shaman leaped down from the post. "I will return to the room," he told them. "Perhaps you two should go eat."

They agreed and headed to the mess hall, where the cooks briefly argued that they were still supposed to be in their rooms before grudgingly serving them a meal of thick beef and vegetable stew, along with buttered cornbread and more hard cider.

"Well," Carl mused, "now that I've had more time to

think it over, I suspect that warhammer was what *really* won you the battle. Swords can't do much against plate armor unless you get a pointy one and thrust it through the armpit or something like that. Bludgeon-type weapons are better. That was why I chose the mace, though since you *weren't* in heavy armor, I might have done better with a sword."

She laughed. "Live and learn. You never know what kind of armor, weapons, magic, or whatever else an opponent is going to have, so it helps to know how to fight in multiple ways."

The thought entered her head that Carl had probably not been briefed about Fenris's involvement. If Balder *had* told him, he had done a fine job of disguising his recognition. Bailey suspected the scion didn't know and legitimately believed that "Marcus" was a regular albeit wise and powerful were-shaman. She'd wait until Fenris gave her permission before she revealed his identity.

They continued to chat over their meal, finally retiring to the manor hall, where Bailey said goodnight to her friend at his door.

He nodded. "Goodnight, yourself. Give me a day or two to recover before we spar again."

"Deal," she acceded, then returned to her room.

Fenris was waiting for her, as she knew he would be.

"Well done," he intoned. "You used a limited form of grounding to weaken him without killing, and you managed a crude deflective shield under pressure. There's work to do on that front, but you have your foot in the door, so to speak."

"Thanks." She sat down, realizing how tired she was, and kicked off her boots.

Fenris stood up from his seat by the fire the same instant she lay back on the bed. Without looking at her, the wolf-god added, "You've done enough for today. Tomorrow, I will be leaving to speak to the council again. Freya needs to be confronted. Not yet with violence, but with the facts of her own foolishness where the other gods can hear. When I see how everyone reacts, I can tell you more."

Bailey turned her head toward him. "You're going alone?"

"Yes." He went to the bookcase and perused the spines. "I'll remain here while you rest for the night, but in the morning, I want you to stay behind and monitor how things go. If they resume the normal training regimen, participate. I won't be long."

She wished the path ahead of them was clearer, but it all depended on Freya—a goddess who seemed exceedingly touchy.

"Have fun," she told her mentor, grimacing.

CHAPTER ELEVEN

Bailey awoke to find the quarantine had been lifted. Normality was returning, though at a slower pace since training for the day seemed to be voluntary. No one had woken her with a trumpet or demanded she rouse herself.

She took her time getting ready and drifting out to the yard, and she bumped into Carl near the door.

"Hey," he greeted her. "They're still in the process of reconfiguring their agenda after all the damage Ragnar caused, but there's limited stuff going on for those who want to participate."

"Well," Bailey quipped, "I'd say we want to. Right? Better than sitting on our asses."

He chuckled and nodded. "Right, indeed."

The girl put her hands on her hips and looked over the walls toward the distant forests. "To be honest, I feel like we've trained enough. What else do they have to teach us? Like, I'm sure they have a program set up, but I don't care much what it is since it's probably nothing we either don't already know or couldn't figure out on our own, or with the help of our mentors. Marcus in my case and I guess Balder in yours."

He pursed his lips, and his dignified face became thoughtful. "You might be right about that. Balder is not the most expressive of gods, but he's knowledgeable and knows when to push me."

"Yeah," said Bailey. "And think about it. Who stopped Ragnar, the trainers? The gods? Nope. It was us, demigods-in-training. Doesn't that mean we have the power and skill we'll need?"

Carl shrugged. He seemed conflicted, as though he agreed with her but didn't want to be obvious about it in case it led him to conclusions that would get him in trouble with his patron.

"Anyway," she murmured, "this isn't such a bad place, and it's good for keeping sharp and meeting new people if nothing else. Besides, I've got people to impress. People and gods. Here, it's nice to be just another trainee for a while. Not a shaman, a werewitch, or even the inheritor of frickin' Aradia's power, but only another newbie going through the motions. It's liberating."

The scion gave her a sad smile. "Sometimes I shapeshift into a random stranger and go places I've never seen before where no one knows who I am, so I understand. But we were sent here because the deities wished it. They seem to be concerned about you. Why else would they have sent me to spy on you?" He laughed.

Scowling, she grumbled, "Good point."

"Running off would look reckless and might rekindle their suspicions," he continued. "So let's go with the flow until further notice. No one thinks you're a threat here, and no one thinks you're special. We're all equal. Dumb neophytes in need of training, like you said. We can spend time honing our skills, cracking skulls, building muscle, and, you know, having fun."

The girl recalled how good it had felt to smash Carl's helmet with her warhammer. "Yeah, you convinced me. Good job. Let's get some food and then talk to the trainers about what they have available."

They had brunch, which consisted of banana bread, yogurt, and tea, then sought out one of the trainers. The nearest man who fit the bill was a short, squinting, rotund individual who looked fearsome but turned out to be surprisingly good-natured.

"Looking for training, are you?" he quipped in a strange accent that sounded like a cross between Irish and Mandarin Chinese. "Well, we're happy to oblige, we are. Got things brewing right now. Of course, there's been plenty of action for everyone's tastes of late with the battles in the castle and the murders and all."

Bailey cracked her neck. "We're ready. I'm looking forward to getting my hands on a weapon."

"No weapons," the trainer chided, and she and Carl both frowned. "Today, you're getting magic lessons."

Fenris stepped out of the portal into a long crystalline hallway, one he'd been in many times before and very recently. He walked down the corridor toward the hazy arch that led to where the deities of the council sat in session.

The wolf-god stepped through the barrier and into the chamber. The councilmembers looked at him with eyes that ranged from flat and neutral to downright suspicious.

Thoth folded his broad dark hands before his face. "Fenris. We did not summon you, but if you have important matters to discuss, we will hear you out. Considering, in particular, your mentorship of Bailey."

The hooded man replied, "There *are* important things we must talk about. Not least the fact that Bailey would be in no condition to be mentored by me, or anyone else, had we not narrowly avoided the consequences of a gross error made by this council."

He did not look at anyone but stared into the bluish-white haze behind the central throne. There was a beat of uncomfortable silence.

Thor, his red brows bristling, rumbled, "What error? And there is always the risk of death during training. You know the dangers involved."

"I do," Fenris returned, "which is how I know this went far beyond the normal risks. Trainees are expected to brave hazardous conditions, but ones that *aren't* expected to kill them unless necessary. Contrast that with having a dangerous and violent man sent with orders to kill her."

Freya and Balder had grown visibly stiff, discomfited. Thor seemed subtly shocked, and Thoth and Coyote were at once aghast and curious. Only Loki looked as though the words had not fazed him.

Grinding her teeth, Freya inquired, "Speak plainly, Fenris. Of what do you accuse us?"

"Dishonesty," he stated, "and incompetence. In your case, especially."

The goddess of witches dug her fingers into the armrests of her chair, and the electrified green light that played about her head grew in intensity.

Fenris continued, "The spy you sent to keep an eye on Bailey was a berserker, one with evidence of being severely disturbed and lacking in the ability to control his blood-lust. He seems to have invented reasons to murder other students, and even a pair of trainers, at random. Then he attacked my pupil, all because you invested him with the power to make his own judgment as to whether she needed to die. A man whose sole purpose in life was to kill! Bailey and a scion named Carl narrowly managed to destroy him. *After* he'd done tremendous damage to the entire operation, that is."

Coyote stared at Freya. "Why in all the universes did you do that?"

"Furthermore," Fenris added before his sister could speak in her defense, "the one named Carl is *another* spy, sent by Balder. He, at least, seems to be sane."

Loki snorted. "The plot has thickened. I thought *I* was the devious one..."

Freya stood up. "Why have you come? *Truly*, Fenris? To challenge me? To announce a full break with the will of this council? To—"

"No," the wolf-father shouted. He kept his calm but raised his voice to its full volume to cut her off. "I have not come to take any drastic action, but simply to reveal the truth so the entire council may assess the matter and act as it deems wise."

Thor spoke up at once. "What *wasn't* wise, Freya, was sending a bearshirt on an undercover reconnaissance mission. What possessed you to do that? Such men are for battles where dozens of men need slaying, not for work that requires sober judgment!"

The Vanir goddess turned to glare at the Æsir god.

Thoth chimed in before she could speak. "I'm afraid I agree. Freya, we've trusted your wisdom thus far, but that was downright stupid on your part."

She sat down, too furious to speak or react.

The Egyptian lord of the occult raised a hand and continued, "It must be said, however, that we—all of us— have been keeping an eye on Bailey. We are concerned about her ability to handle the amount of power she possesses, but we haven't sent proxies to spy on her."

"Aye!" Thor reiterated. "That smacks of devious plots, I say. We have stuck to watching when we can or asking people in the know. If we make a play, everyone shall know of it openly!"

Coyote shook his head. "Alas, so many godlings full of potential and promise died for no good reason. This council has much to answer for by allowing such a thing to transpire."

"And," Thoth went on, "sending agents after Bailey comes perilously close to direct interference in mortal affairs. Something must be done."

Silence reigned for what felt like far too long.

Freya, resembling a bomb prepared to go off, asked in a soft voice, "What?"

No one offered any immediate solutions except Fenris.

"Perhaps," he suggested, "Freya should step down from the council. At least for a time."

"*What?*" she screamed. "How dare you!"

Balder too balked at the notion, joining his fellow Asgardian in protesting such a move. Both argued that removing Freya would throw off the council's delicate balance.

Thor shrugged, seemingly annoyed with the debate. Though he'd been among the first to agree that Freya had made a bad choice, the whole discussion left a sour taste in his mouth.

Loki, for his part, laughed at the bickering around him. So much chaos clearly amused him.

Coyote and Thoth agreed with the basic wisdom of Fenris's proposal but quickly turned to disagreement over the merits of how best to implement it.

Freya projected her voice above the general chatter. "Don't trust him!" she announced. "Fenris has a plan, make no mistake. He means to meddle, to advance upon us from an oblique angle!"

Scratching his beard, Thor admitted, "Possibly."

Fenris interrupted, "No, I only seek to protect my disciple, my people, and the stability of the world they live on." But by the time he'd spoken, further squabbles had erupted. He frowned, realizing that none of the council thought him trustworthy. Their differences of temperament and opinion divide them, but they were united in suspecting him of...something.

"Prove it," he shouted at them all. "If I am guilty of playing you false, display your evidence of my crimes!"

None of them could. Instead, they kept arguing.

Roland sipped his coffee. He'd ordered a very nice-looking platter of pasta primavera and preferred to admire it a moment before he started eating. Dante, meanwhile, had received a crude but appetizing-looking plate of fish and chips.

Roland spoke first. "Since I'm closer to Portland, I'll take the responsibility of checking on our friend Megan in a few days."

"That's fair," Dante agreed as he salted his fries.

Upon returning to the woman's occult supply store, the two wizards had presented her with an ultimatum: leave the Pacific Northwest immediately, go as far away as possible, and don't come back. In return, they would not inform the families of the missing witches that she'd been complicit in their deaths. She had, after all, been blackmailed by a caster of superior power, but they refused to let her off the hook entirely.

"The important thing," Roland remarked, "is that we neutralized you-know-who. That's two down, one to go."

Dante gave him an odd glance.

"Never mind," the older wizard said, waving his hand. "There were three of them—my stalkers. I have yet to see or hear from the third. With any luck, she took a long vacation to Antarctica."

The younger caster swallowed his food and rolled his shoulders. "In any event, we handled this whole thing cleanly. If it had gone on much longer, witches might have started blaming each other, or worse, they might have blamed the Weres. I don't want the peace we've created to get fucked up."

Roland finally picked up his fork. "No sane person does."

A car pulled up outside the diner, its blinding electric-blue lights shining straight through the window. Once the lights, along with the engine, died, the vehicle itself was clearly visible—an elongated black Maybach. The doors opened, and out stepped two men in dark suits and glasses.

Roland sighed and tilted his head back, looking at the ceiling. "Now what?"

Dante wiped his mouth. "Uh-oh. Them showing up usually means trouble, even when they're on our side."

The agents pushed their way into the restaurant and came toward the booth where the wizards sat. Roland recognized one as Velasquez, the new leader of the task force that had helped them take on Aradia. The other was an Asian guy he hadn't seen before. He understood that Townsend was still recovering.

"Hello," Velasquez said. Before the casters could reply, he and his partner sat down on both sides of the booth, forcing Roland and Dante to scooch inwards and blocking them from making an easy exit. "We need to talk," the agent added.

Roland nodded. "It's nice to see you again too, dear. And my, aren't you looking lovely!"

Ignoring the comment, Velasquez gestured at the newcomer. "This is Agent Park, my new partner. We know who you are, and we remember the services you've done for the United States. We still have to ask what you two are doing in Portland."

Dante stroked his hair. "It's partway between our hometowns. We hadn't seen each other in a while and wanted to hang out and have a nice meal. We almost succeeded."

Agent Park snorted. "You're right about the 'nice meal' part. Is that Alaskan cod?"

Dante blinked in confusion.

Velasquez butted back in, getting straight to business. "That's obviously bullshit, given the coincidences involved. Our intel informs us that several witches have gone missing. Not huge numbers of them, but enough to be of concern. With you guys and the furballs getting along so splendidly lately, *and* the Venatori lying low, who the fuck could be responsible? We're curious."

Roland countered, "You assumed we would know?"

"Sure," Park shot back, grinning broadly. "I'm new, but I read your file. You're a leader. If you sucked, maybe you wouldn't know, but it sounds like you've got too much on the ball to be caught totally unaware by something like this."

Roland made a pouty face. "Gosh. I guess I *do* suck, then."

Dante snickered at that.

Waving a hand sharply, Velasquez snapped, "Enough with the smartassery. We also know Bailey has mysteriously vanished again, at a time when *supposedly* nothing is wrong. That seems a little strange. You know we're not your enemies. We're on the same side. Don't make things difficult for us, and we can keep being friends."

The wizards sighed, and Roland turned to Velasquez after taking another swig of coffee. "Fine. We heard about the missing witches, so we investigated. The situation has been resolved."

"Details," demanded Velasquez.

The casters reluctantly filled the agents in on all that had happened.

"And of course," Roland elaborated as they neared the end of the story, "it turned out it was Caldoria McCluskey, who I'm sure you also have a file on, seeing as she and her girlfriends were the ones who basically started the entire mess involving Bailey and me. We thought she got lost or killed in the Other, but wraiths of some sort got hold of her and turned her into this undead hag-like creature who needed to drain the powers and life force of other witches to restore herself. Meaning that yes, the people she kidnapped are dead."

Dante added, "We dusted her, though. Tired her out and then blasted her into oblivion. All should be well from here on."

In the middle of the wizards' account, Velasquez had pulled out a small laptop and begun keying in information. With the story done, he hit the Enter key, apparently checking a database Roland suspected was exclusive to the Agency.

The agent shook his head and let out a dry, sardonic chuckle devoid of humor. "There's one little problem with the end of your story," he observed.

"True," Roland admitted, "we forgot to craft a clever punchline."

As Park watched with a grim expression, Velasquez turned the screen toward the wizards. "What you had there was what we call an eldritch crone, kind of a magically empowered super zombie. They're rare but serious business. There's no way you destroyed one that easily."

Dante scoffed. "It wasn't what I'd call easy, exactly, and there wasn't anything left of her."

Velasquez adjusted his glasses. "Maybe you destroyed her body, but not her spirit. I would've thought this would have occurred to you guys, being sorcerers and all. She's probably still out there in incorporeal form, siphoning bits of magic from other witches until she has the strength to reconstitute a physical body, though it'd be a frail and feeble husk until she could absorb more victims. That would be enough for her to move and cause problems."

"So," Park surmised, "we need to find her—or it, whatever—and stop her. Again."

Roland held up a hand. "Let me eat, then we'll be happy to help. I can't magically track anything worth a damn on an empty stomach."

"Make it fast," ordered Velasquez. "We have tracking capabilities of our own, though. Finish your meals and come with us. We'll show you the hardware, then we're all going on a hunt."

Bailey and Carl sat cross-legged, facing one another on a circular patch of dirt in the middle of the forest. Tall trees and dense foliage surrounded them so that they felt as though they were at the bottom of a dark-green cylinder.

Their trainer for the current exercise was a stern-looking woman who had introduced herself as Deona. As if sensing the first questions her students were on the verge of asking, she cut them off with a curt explanation.

"Sitting is preferred when one is a beginner at illusion

magic. It requires tremendous amounts of control and mastery, which is why we're teaching you this first. Should you feel that conjuring illusions is of little value in and of itself, be aware that the effort that goes into learning it will improve your overall latent divine abilities and condition you to accept extra physical and magical strain."

Bailey nodded. Fenris had adopted a similar philosophy in his many lessons with her.

Carl looked more skeptical. "I'm a shapeshifter," he pointed out. "My body can take on most any appearance I want. This seems redundant, in all honesty."

"As I said," Deona repeated, her tone growing harder-edged, "the exercise itself will be beneficial. The ability to alter your form is not the same thing as being able to create external images and sounds."

He scowled but offered no further protest.

The trainer went on, "Neither of you is in immediate danger, yet the godly magical ability lying within you and not subject to discipline can eat away at you like a cancer. In rare cases, it may burst like an overfilled balloon. With power like yours, the results of that would be much like an atomic explosion. I hardly need to add that this is best avoided."

"Yeah," Bailey conceded, "sounds about right."

They began with Deona walking them through the gradual process of creating mental images, then projecting them into the outside world. First they did easy stuff like spheres and cubes, and the trainees found that even simple shapes required constant mental attention to maintain.

Bailey kept her mind on the act of controlling the holograph, but her eyes drifted to the sphere. It was convincing, like a real object. She hadn't quite nailed the lighting, though, since it was illuminated as if it floated in a white room with panoramic illumination rather than a shadowy thicket.

Then Deona commanded them to mirror the image. To replicate it exactly, creating a second while maintaining the first.

They did, though it took a moment, and Bailey felt the strain increasing. It *was* a workout, taxing her mental and magical capabilities in the same way her arms would be strained by holding a heavy suitcase at chest height.

"Double them," said the trainer. "Turn the two into four. Think of the pair as a single dual unit that must be replicated once. That is far more efficient than trying to create more than one at a time."

It was easier than Bailey had thought it would be, though she grew tired and had to concentrate hard.

Deona continued to supervise them as they doubled the doubles, the number of shapes multiplying at an exponential rate until the clearing was crowded with phantom spheres and cubes.

"Good," the trainer praised them. "Now dismiss them. This concludes the first part of the lesson."

The shapes vanished and Bailey and Carl reeled in place, breathing heavily and rubbing their eyes.

The scion looked up. "Did you say, 'first part?'"

Deona smirked. "Yes."

Next they repeated the same procedure, but with illusory images of themselves. Carl seemed mildly unnerved by having his doppelganger hover before him, but Bailey shrugged it off. During her exercises in the Other, she'd been forced to confront malevolent mirror images of herself on at least three different occasions.

Their trainer showed them how to bind the illusions to themselves and control their movements and speech. There was no way to automate the process; it required active effort on the students' part.

Deona waved a hand at their handiwork. "In doing this, you are using your abilities in creatively subtle ways while controlling a large amount of powerful magic. It bleeds off excess arcane energy while acclimating you to the use of what you possess."

The trainer ordered them to stand up and face their doubles. She instructed them in the process of "programming" the illusions to go through certain rote motions and then routines or combinations of activities, essentially turning them into sparring robots.

"Well," the werewitch murmured under her breath, "guess I won't need a partner anymore." Her illusory clone swung a series of punches at her and she blocked them and struck back, punching her double in the gut and shoving her away.

Carl shook his head. "This is uncanny, isn't it? I'm used to being someone else, but never while leaving an extra copy of myself behind."

Deona had them set their illusions against each other in a mock battle, each trainee sitting at the edge of the circle and acting as puppet master to their doppelganger. The mental and magical strain increased. Each caster struggled to exert a finer level of control over their conjuration, translating their personal combat skills into talent at manipulating the double.

To Bailey's irritation, Carl won four out of five matches. "We'll need a rematch, you realize," she told him.

He shrugged. "I suppose this comes naturally after getting past the initial weirdness."

The sunlight faded, and near dusk, Deonna finally called a halt.

"Good," she said. "You would both benefit from further practice, but you've done well and made significant progress. Return to your quarters and rest. Today's lesson is concluded."

They thanked her and walked back through the trees, crossing the grassy moor toward the castle as day gave way to night.

Bailey chuckled to herself. "It's weird; we spent most of our time sitting, aside from the part where we fought the illusions ourselves, but I feel like I spent the whole damn day running and lifting weights."

"Me too," Carl agreed. "Nothing quite like that feeling of being done with an extensive workout and getting to relax."

"Yeah." Bailey looked into the distance, her face wistful. "It'd be nice if the mess hall served cold beer, though."

CHAPTER TWELVE

A s he sat in the incredibly comfortable backseat of the Maybach, Roland sighed, "I have to admit, I'm impressed. Not only with the ride, but with the rest of the hardware. I didn't think Americans paid enough taxes to finance all of this."

Agent Park, in the front passenger seat, laughed out loud, but Velasquez just shook his head. "There are ways," the senior agent muttered. "You don't want to know."

"You're right," agreed Roland instantly. "I don't."

Next to him, Dante had been allowed to man the tracking device. It looked like a tablet with a couple of odd protrusions on it, one of which glowed bright green when they picked up a signal.

It was glowing again.

Dante exclaimed, "We're getting something! It's pretty close, too. Didn't creep up on us, so either it dropped straight down out of the sky or came up from the sewers. Or it might have teleported out of an alternate dimension."

The agents had a small display screen on their dashboard that mirrored the results on the tracker, so they were able to see the pertinent information without having to rely on Dante to describe it to them.

"Good," said Velasquez. He spun the wheel to the left, taking them down a side street off the major road they'd been cruising on. The businesses and residences of Portland fell away in the electric glare that dispelled much of nighttime's gloom.

Roland leaned over the device in Dante's hands, watching the interactive map move on the screen as the green dot they were following made its way through the city.

Dante blinked. "Whoa, yeah, she's moving faster but also getting closer to street level. And…wait, she's slowing down again."

Glancing up, Roland saw that the agents were following a faint blue trail in the air, not unlike the tracking spell he'd once cast on a vehicle to help Bailey follow it.

"Hey," he asked, "are we *supposed* to be able to see where the spirit-thing went? I thought you said it was invisible. Or is this some trickery of yours?"

"Trickery," Park answered him. "When I heard this thing would be my wheels, I looked into it. Turns out we've got an advanced HUD in the windows that picks up on spectral energy and otherworldly entities. Cool, right?"

The wizard nodded. "Let me know when it hits the civilian market. Need I remind you that this particular spectral entity used to *stalk* me personally?"

Velasquez muttered, "You mentioned it eight or nine times. Shit, she's heading toward the caster nightclubs. Why am I not surprised?"

Dante offered, "Well, that's where the witches are. She needs to go where the food will be."

Another three or four minutes of driving brought them near one of the clubs Roland and Dante had visited in their search for Megan's New Age supply shop. A crowd of young witches split almost evenly between males and females was gathered outside the front entrance.

Velasquez brought the Maybach to a stop across the street and perhaps four hundred feet away. "The scanner," he said, and Park opened a compartment to pull out another handheld device that looked like a clear flat square screen about 8" in all dimensions mounted on a pistol handle.

Everyone piled out of the vehicle, Dante reminding them that the phantasmal entity had come to a stop slightly above the club.

As the wizards watched, Agent Park held up the scanner, revealing a translucent blob of blue light floating in midair over the heads of the oblivious clubgoers. Roland shuddered. The ghost-thing looked an awful lot like a withered crone dressed in wispy rags, yet strangely, it was still recognizable as Callie.

"Okay," Roland began, as he and Dante prepared spells, "this is a witch district anyway, so we'll—"

Velasquez cut him off. "*No*, you won't. Regardless of what type of district it is, it's still too goddamn public to go throwing magic around. Let us handle this."

Roland watched the scene before them. He could see little tendrils of arcane power wafting up from the young men and women by the entrance like steam, being absorbed by the ravenous apparition. It seemed that Callie, as revealed by the scanner, grew brighter and more substantial, and the witches beneath her began to stumble or wipe their brows or lean against lampposts.

"Shit," he heard one girl say, "I feel really weak all of a sudden."

Velasquez and Park grabbed weapons from another compartment within the car. They reminded Roland of pump-action squirt guns plated in chrome, paired with small opaque wrist-mounted tanks.

Dante snorted. "So we can't use magic in a place where lots of magic-users hang out, but you guys can fire guns? 'Murica."

Park bit down on a laugh. Velasquez replied, "Yeah, yeah, cute. These things fire invisible beams that disrupt the static fields that hold arcanoplasmic masses together, meaning they'll paralyze our floating undead friend there long enough for us to vacuum up her halves."

Roland shuddered. "Halves? You guys are making me feel like a dumbass. How is it that there's all this supernatural shit I'd never heard about? Ugh."

"Life force in one tank," said Park, "arcane energy in the other."

"That way," Velasquez added, "she can't reconstitute herself in any capacity—living, undead, corporeal, or spectral—and will be helpless until we can dissipate the energy and destroy her life essence for good."

Roland waved a hand. "Sounds awesome. Do your thing, boys."

The agents took aim.

"Wait," blurted Dante, who was watching through the scanner, but he was too late. Callie had noticed them at the last instant, and she shot upwards. Roland saw tiny lights flash on the sides of the agents' guns, but nothing appeared to happen in the real world. Seen through the scanner, though, two blazing bolts of green light streaked toward the specter but passed harmlessly through the empty air where it had been.

"Dammit!" Velasquez exclaimed. Callie was halfway down the street and gaining speed.

Roland put a hand over his eyes. *They should have let us blast her. We're used to containing our enemies while we fight so we don't have to bother with leading the target.*

The senior agent waved an arm and jumped into the driver's seat. "Back in the car."

They all obeyed, and the chase continued.

Fenris hadn't budged, but he had not made much progress either, since each time he tried to turn the discussion to Freya's competence, the other gods twisted it back to the subject of *Bailey's* competence.

Freya shouted, "Look at all the chaos that's followed her. There's no peace around the girl, even at the training grounds, where such things are not supposed to happen! She must have done something to antagonize Ragnar."

Fenris struggled to control his temper. "Utter nonsense. Self-control has been the focus of her instruction since I first met her."

Thoth raised a hand to silence them both. "How has she fared thus far, aside from the incident with the berserker? Has she in truth demonstrated proper behavior and restraint? We've not yet heard back from the trainers."

"That," Fenris grated, "is because they're too busy cleaning up the mess left by Freya's agent, who Bailey was able to subdue with help from Carl, the scion. At present, she's chosen to remain to further her training for the safety of all, and out of respect for this council's wishes. Is that respect returned to her?"

Balder cleared his throat. "That is a specious comparison," he stated in his soft, pleasant voice, "since she is merely—"

"A goddess," Fenris finished. "In power, and soon to be one in wisdom and discipline as well. When that day comes, as it soon shall, will she be acknowledged?" He paused, absorbing the stares of the others. "What awaits her? How shall she be received when she's cleared every hurdle placed before her? She's cleared most of them already."

Coyote scratched behind a pointed ear. "Hmm. It depends on many things, Fenris, but I understand what you mean. Ultimately, the girl must be given the same chance as anyone else."

The wolf-father raised a fist into the air. "So you say, Coyote, but will the council's actions reflect your sentiment? From day one, Bailey has been treated as a threat, a *presumed* loose cannon or potential usurper of some sort, yet her actions have contradicted that presumption time and again. After she's completed her training, will she receive recognition of her full godhood? Will she get a mantle, a portfolio? Will she be offered a seat in this conclave?"

The council deities fidgeted, averted their eyes, or glared. Conversation drew to a close as all of them contemplated the implications of what Fenris had said.

He was not shocked to see that Freya was the most upset of the six. She looked like she might launch herself from her chair and lock her fingers around his throat, but she did not.

"So," she said instead, "you've been training her to take my place? Is that it?"

"No," he replied, keeping his voice calm, "but now that you bring it up, perhaps it demonstrates that the question has been on your mind. Since I've proposed that you should temporarily retire from presiding here, why not a test? A challenge to see who sits in that chair?"

Thor leaned forward. "What? What kind of a test, Fenris?"

"Yes," Thoth added, "what are you suggesting?"

The wolf-god breathed deep as his sister's eyes bored holes through his heart.

"I suggest a contest or a trial be put before Bailey after she's graduated, the prize being that seat, at least for a time. If Bailey wins, Freya must step down, and my protege must be mantled with the divine dignity she has earned and have a say in how things are run to go with her newfound responsibilities as well as her powers. This is how such things have always been done. Will the council agree to a fair shot, or are you only heckling her because you *can* and resent the ascension of a mortal?"

Everyone tried to speak at once, and the pandemonium lasted several heartbeats. Finally, Thor leapt up on his chair and bellowed, *"Silence! Shut up, all of you!"*

Since his voice was the loudest, the others' protestations fell off.

Thoth stood up. "We shall put it to a vote."

Freya scoffed. "You're seriously considering listening to him?" She swept a hand toward Fenris. "He wants his apprentice to sit on this council as a foot in the door to advance whatever his agenda is. You all know it!"

Balder frowned but agreed with Thoth. "Yes, let us vote. Reason should win out at the end, dear sister."

Watching the six council members, Fenris tried not to smile. "We shall see."

The mall would be closing in less than an hour, but it was surprisingly busy.

"Turn right," Dante shouted, still holding the tracking device in his hands. He kept his eyes on it most of the time and only snapped up his gaze every few seconds to make sure he wasn't about to run into a person or a potted tree.

He, along with Roland and Agents Velasquez and Park, jogged through the halls of a vast shopping establishment that lay only three blocks from the nightclub where they'd failed to capture Callie.

The eldritch crone, desperate for power and sustenance, had vanished into the nearest place where large numbers of witches could be expected to gather. At first, Velasquez had cursed their poor luck. They couldn't drive into the mall, obviously, and it was big enough for the specter to cross to the other side and be gone before the Maybach could drive around the periphery.

But Dante had noticed something as he'd followed the tracking screen. Callie seemed to be staying within the confines of the walls, even when it would have made more sense for her to cut through them.

Park snapped his fingers. "She's solidifying. The reaction must have been delayed, but I bet she absorbed enough magic and life force from those witches by the club that she's beginning to take physical form again."

As they chased her through the structure, they decided Park was right. She couldn't be seen with the naked eye, not exactly. What they saw was a vague cloud of dust, combined with patches of air where the light and shadows didn't seem quite right. Viewed through the scanner, though, she was a shambling skeletal form dressed in rags made of dirt and moss.

Dante brushed against a girl who shouted, "Hey!" and glared after him, but there was no time to apologize. He was lagging in the rear of the formation. He considered himself to be in good shape, but he could not keep up with the others, especially Park, who had come to the Agency straight from the military and could probably have run a marathon before breakfast.

The young wizard looked through the scanner, which Velasquez was manning. They saw a blue-tinted ragged form disappear through a door ahead, around the corner leading to the mostly-abandoned food court.

Roland said, "It's an overstock room for the restaurants. Don't think she can get out that way. Might try to ambush us, though."

"Whatever," Velasquez snapped. "Get her!"

They bolted ahead and threw open the door, finding

themselves in a dark space which, though large, was crowded with shelving, boxes, and tubs.

Dante suggested, "Leave the lights off. She might not be able to see us any better than we can see her. She's been moving more by feel than sight, I think."

The senior agent grunted. "You may be right."

Roland cringed. "That's spooky. Callie jumping out at me from a dark corner is something I never, ever want to happen."

The scanner revealed only blackness as Velasquez panned it around, and they tried to make as little sound as they could, slowly advancing inward. Something crashed.

The agents pivoted and the scanner revealed...nothing. Then, in the scanner, Dante saw a faint blue glow past their shoulders.

"Behind you!" he shouted, and Velasquez dropped the tracking device.

Both wizards raised their hands and collaboratively conjured a shield that saved the two agents from death. A roaring cloud of poisoned ice shards dissipated against the arcane barrier.

Velasquez and Park spun, drawing their weapons and firing. The scanner showed the hideous image of the phantom hag, half-ghost and half-zombie, snarling at them as the green beams converged on her. Her dead eyes widened.

"Roland!" she cried out in a rasping hiss. Then the beams struck her in the chest, and her form wavered and dissolved.

Velasquez said, "Now!" and he and his partner deployed their suction tanks. One glowed green and one magenta;

faint streams of glimmering blue dust were vacuumed into each, then silence set in.

Park laughed. "I might end up liking this job after all."

Roland simply wiped his brow and leaned against a shelf. Dante wondered if hearing the creature call his name had been more than he could take. He'd known her, after all.

The four men exited the storeroom, whistling casually in case security spotted them, and left the mall through the food court's doors to make the long walk back to their car.

Velasquez turned to the wizards. "Thank you for helping us in general, and for saving our asses in there. We have a file on eldritch crones, but neither of us has fought one before, so we didn't know what to expect. In any event, she's no threat to anyone, broken down into her essential salts or whatever. We'll give you a ride back to that diner, then we'll get rid of her once and for all. We promise."

"Comforting," said Roland.

Dante looked down at the tracking device. After he'd picked it back up in the storeroom, he'd forgotten to check it till now, and Park joined him in examining it.

"Jesus," the agent muttered. "The screen's cracked."

Dante shrugged. "Well, don't worry. The taxpayers will foot the bill. Right?"

CHAPTER THIRTEEN

Fenris had refused to leave until the council voted, and as he'd reminded them, any time he spent here was time he wasn't spending watching over Bailey.

"So be it," Thoth said at last, and aside from Freya, the others agreed. "We shall vote on whether Bailey should at least be brought in to defend herself while advancing her case as per the Ragnar incident."

The council decided six to one to accept Fenris's suggestion.

"Fools," Freya said through gritted teeth. "You will come to regret this nonsense."

The Egyptian deity, who usually acted as spokesperson and mediator for the council as a whole, tried to calm her down. "We have not voted to depose you at this time, Freya, only to hear the girl's side of the story. Then we'll go from there."

"Aye," Thor rumbled. "We've plotted behind her back enough as it is. I'd feel remiss if she wasn't present to give her own account. We're not such *nithlings* as to backstab her, are we?"

Coyote added, "The idea, I think, is not to bring her here for direct confrontation or combat, but simply a reckoning. Bailey and Freya should discuss their differences and present their reasons for acting as they have. Such a talk could be productive. Then we can move on to further judgments if need be."

Thoth nodded. "Yes, I agree. The werewitch will not yet be judged, but she will be tested by each of us individually by fair standards to determine her overall worth and integrity. It is rare for a newly-ascended divinity to supplant a well-established one, but not unheard of. Freya, there is a good chance that you will retain your seat, but given your recent error, we are forced to consider Fenris's proposal."

Rather than respond to the Egyptian, Freya turned to the wolf-god.

"So, Fenris," she began, "the council is in agreement that Bailey will be evaluated by us directly. If we go forward with this course of action, you are committing your pupil to the possibility of rejection and failure. Do you agree to subject her to that?"

Fenris ignored his sister's obvious and arrogant implications. "So be it. Normally I leave major decisions in her hands, but in this case, it seems I must speak for her. I hereby pledge her participation in your trials and put her at the mercy of your wisdom."

Freya smiled. "Good."

Bailey ran down the dirt path. Beside her, a second Bailey ran in perfect synchronization with her movements. Both werewitches advanced with the same steady long-legged stride. Each breathed in time with the other. Their hair flapped in the breeze as if in a mirror, and when a log trap fell in front of them, both reflexively jumped over it and rolled past, then sprang back into a jog.

It was late morning. Bailey had risen early, getting breakfast and stretching and washing out of the way before heading to the obstacle course alone. She wanted to run through it again, taking different paths than the ones she'd used previously. While she was at it, she figured she could stand to practice illusion magic.

The training grounds were not quite ready to resume normal operations, and activities were still on an elective basis. Bailey had briefly spoken to Deona, and the woman had told her they expected the usual program to resume tomorrow.

She was approximately halfway through the course, and she was damn tired. Maintaining the illusion and ensuring that it remained connected to her and did exactly what she did doubled the effort she had to put into everything else the course threw at her.

She wondered if Carl had tagged along. He'd waffled, wanting to give himself a day to catch up on scholarly pursuits, but he'd suggested he might follow her into the course a bit later.

Minutes later, Bailey spotted the scion advancing toward a point where two paths converged. He must have entered the run directly behind her to be so close.

"Hey!" she shouted, and her clone mouthed the word

also. "What's a lowlife like you doing in a classy place like this?"

"Silence," he shouted back. "This place isn't classy *at all*. Wait, which one of you am I speaking to?"

Laughing, she pulled ahead of him. "You'll have to figure that out on your own."

Then something about the quality of his footfalls changed, and when she glanced over her shoulder again, two Carls ran behind her. Being taller, he was gaining on her.

"You asked for it," he said, though she was uncertain which had spoken. Probably the one on the left.

The path narrowed and began to ascend a rocky slope, and Bailey slowed just enough for the scion and his double to nearly crash into her.

She snapped, "That's it. As soon as this path widens, it's go-time for all four of us. You owe me a rematch from last night anyway."

He voiced no objection. They crested the ridge and came to a wide plain filled with tall, swaying emerald grass and mossy stones.

Carl and his clone attacked without preamble. Bailey had expected him to say something first, but she was used to having to fight on little notice, and she had a shield up in time to block the scions' dual fireball attacks.

She conjured a ward then, one that would absorb water-based spells. He wouldn't likely try fire twice, and during their armored duel she'd warded herself against electricity, so it made sense to her that he'd attempt something different.

With the ward up, she sent a flurry of tiny pebbles at

the pair, noticing how they passed through the figure on the right. That was obviously the illusion. She commanded her double to engage it while she took on the real Carl.

I have the advantage this time, she thought as she ducked and pivoted around Carl's melee attacks. *He's a good fighter, but nobody's better than I am, and all my clone has to do is imitate me.*

She ducked under Carl's arm and elbowed him in the ribs while kicking his legs out from under him. As he fell, he tried to summon a geyser of water beneath her feet, but it dissipated into vapor before it touched her.

She laughed, then turned to throw a lightning bolt at the legs of Carl's double. It struck true, and the illusion flickered while her doppelganger pummeled it. The second Carl fizzled out of existence.

Both Baileys converged on the real scion, flanking him with blindingly fast attacks. Her clone was caught in a net of arcane flame that disintegrated it, but by then, Bailey was able to grab Carl in a headlock and hold a plasma blade to his throat.

"Ughhh." He sighed raggedly. "You win. I'm still better at pure illusion versus illusion combat until further notice."

"Yeah, yeah," she muttered, allowing him to regain his feet. "We'll see about that. Anyway, it was a close fight."

He agreed that it had been a hell of a match, and they finished the course together, crossing the finish line within seconds of one another.

"Man," Carl breathed, "running that much *and* fighting is no joke, is it? I think I need a lunch break."

Bailey thought about joining him but decided to keep

training. "I'll catch up with you later this evening," she promised. They shook hands and went their separate ways.

As the scion headed toward the mess hall, Bailey made for the forest copse where Deona had instructed the two of them yesterday. She found the circle of dirt, sat, and summoned another alternate version of herself.

Then, breathing deep and concentrating, she employed the doubling technique to create two, four, and finally eight extra Baileys. Each time, the relative effort required was less, yet the cumulative strain of maintaining that many of them was enough so she could only do it for five or ten minutes at first.

She tried again, resting for a short while and then re-summoning the eight illusions. This time she stood up and again commanded them to shadow and imitate her. She jogged around the woods and leapt over fallen trees here and there, and drilled basic fighting moves.

The clones followed her with minimal errors for what felt like half an hour or so before she had to release them into oblivion. Then she sat, sweaty and winded, on a lichen-covered log, admiring the beauty of the woods.

Seven paces from her position, a glowing purple doorway opened in the air, and out stepped a tall man wearing a hooded coat.

"Fenris, you made it back," she greeted him. "Hope things went okay back in Shiny Crystal Land. Things are pretty okay here. I was getting some more training in."

The wolf-father smiled gently. "I was watching you from afar. You've grown by leaps and bounds in the brief time we've known each other—half a mortal year or less— and you continue to impress me. Each time you face a challenge, you set yourself a goal and push through to the next stage in your evolution. I'm proud of you."

She felt like she was melting inside, hearing that, in a good way. She walked over and gave him a hug. "Thanks, old man. Couldn't have done it without you."

"Perhaps not," he acknowledged. "But you've been a good student. Keep it up, and in no time, you will have perfect control over your new stores of magic. Managing so much power will be as natural to you as breathing."

"That's the hope," she quipped. "So, uh, did Freya resign her post, or..."

His expression grew serious. "Not quite, but we'll talk more of that later. Nothing terrible or drastic has happened, but something's come up, and since the training grounds are still recovering from their losses, I feel we might take a short leave of absence."

She separated from him and squinted. "To go where?"

"Home," he stated. Turning, he dismissed the portal he'd come through and opened another in its stead. "Please, follow me. The trainers will not give you any trouble for taking one day off at a time when it's permissible to do so."

Though she looked forward to seeing Greenhearth and her family and pack again, she hesitated, thinking it would be better to tell Carl and the trainers first. Then she shrugged and stepped into the gateway.

After the customary rush of dizzying cold, she emerged on the familiar pine-covered slopes of Oregon with her equally familiar pole barn, backyard, and house before her. It was mid-afternoon, and the day was warm, muggy, and partially cloudy.

Kurt was standing at the edge of the yard, facing away

from her and taking a leak against a tree while he whistled to himself and looked into the mountains.

Bailey waited till it looked like he was mostly done pissing before she shouted, *"Hi, Kurt!"* at the top of her lungs.

"Shit!" he shrieked, stumbling forward as he struggled to zip his pants up, then twisted around to see her and Fenris. He blinked. "Oh. Uh, yeah, hi. What are you doing back so soon?"

Bailey cracked up, and Fenris bowed his head and chuckled a bit. The back door opened, and Jacob and Russell appeared.

"The hell?" Jacob asked. "Hi, Bailey, glad you're okay. What was that scream?"

Kurt fumed. "Nothing. She startled me. It happens to the best of us."

Jacob nodded. "The best of us, yeah. And also you."

"Shut up." The youngest brother stormed past the other two into the house, presumably to wash his hands and check his underwear.

Bailey looked at Jacob and Russell. "Back on a break. Could use a home-cooked meal instead of all that magical food they've been tossing at us. Oh, and a shower. They're operating at a fourteenth-century tech level in that place, so I've had to scrub myself with water from a damn pitcher."

Russell said, "I thought you smelled different."

She shook her head. "'Different' is probably the polite way of putting it. Anyway, what's for dinner?"

"Not sure yet," Jacob replied, "but we'll come up with something good. Come on in and tell us how things've been going. Oh, by the way, Roland took off to Portland to meet up with his friend. That little gothy dude, I forget his name."

Bailey snapped her fingers. "Dante. Okay, well, I hope they're having a good time or whatever." She tried to hide her disappointment. Now that she was home, it struck her how much she missed Roland.

They all decided they were too hungry to spend a lot of time cooking, so they simply tossed a couple of frozen lasagnas into the oven. The hour it took them to bake would give Bailey time to clean up and talk things over with her brothers.

While she showered, Fenris confided in the three. "Bailey is doing well in her training. There are no problems there. She's performing as well as I expected, if not better."

Jacob laughed into his beer. "Sounds accurate."

"There's more," Fenris added, "but I would rather wait until she is present. She does not yet know everything. I will return shortly."

Kurt screwed up his face. "You going back to Mount Olympus?"

"No," the wolf-god replied, "up the hill. I don't like lasagna."

He walked out the front door and bounded up the slopes into the woods. When he returned forty minutes later, his breath smelled faintly of blood.

The five sat down at the dining room table, pouring Jacob's semi-strong coffee into mugs as they waited for their meal to finish cooking.

Bailey kicked off the ensuing discussion. "All right, first of all," she explained to her siblings, "some crazy guy tried to kill me, but we—me and a friend of mine—took him out. I'm sorry," she went on as her brothers tensed up, "but trouble always seems to find me. Shitty-ass thing since he seemed like a decent guy at first."

Jacob asked, "Why did he try to kill you?"

Fenris jumped in, explaining that the man was a disturbed berserker who wasn't qualified for the excess trust and power Freya had invested him with.

"Wait," Kurt pointed out, "didn't Freya show up in town a while back and make a truce with you? Why's she being such a bitch now? Sorry, Bailey."

The girl shrugged. "She's earning the use of that word if you ask me."

"I don't know," said Fenris. "I suspect it has to do with the pantheon resenting the ascent of a mortal such as Bailey to their level. That leads us to the next thing we must discuss. I spoke to the other gods about these incidents, and they agreed that Freya made a serious error and that Bailey should be given a chance to prove herself."

Bailey inquired, "Yeah, but isn't that what I'm already doing?"

The wolf-father shook his head. "Beyond that. They want you to appear before them, relate your account of all that's happened, and then submit to trials and tests posed by each of them. Including Freya, who stands to lose her seat if you succeed."

The girl whistled. "That sounds like serious shit."

Jacob put a hand on her arm. "You deal well with serious shit. But are these the kind of trials that might kill her, Fenris? We were hoping we wouldn't have to keep worrying whether she's coming home or not every time she leaves."

"I cannot say," the god replied. "The more level-headed among them will ensure that the tests are fair by their standards, but it will be up to each individual to define that term."

Kurt and Russell both snorted.

"Oh," the former remarked in a sarcastic tone, waving his arms, "so they can define 'fair' however they want. That means Freya can ask Bailey to go back in time and change history so she was never born and call it good."

"Not quite," Fenris elaborated, "but I'm sure she'll set a difficult challenge. And they demanded that I answer on your behalf, Bailey. I told them you'd be willing to submit to their tests, but you might be able to back out if you don't feel up to it."

The girl bit her lip. "You know damn well that backing out isn't my thing, though I'll admit I'd rather you'd asked me first. I'll do it, and one way or another, I'll win."

Fenris smiled. "That is exactly what I thought you'd say."

"But," Bailey qualified, "not right away. They're immortals, so there's no need to hurry. I'd like to spend the evening here at home."

"That's fine." The wolf-father pushed back his chair and stood up at the same moment the oven timer went off. "I will see myself out. There are small things I can do to help ensure you have a fighting chance. Call me when you're ready. I will hear you."

He and his protege clasped hands, then he left the house, vanishing into the wooded hills again.

Jacob prodded Kurt in the arm with the butt-end of a fork. "Get the lasagna, dumbass," he ordered.

"Okay," said Gunney, wiping his hands on a dirty rag, "open it up, and let's evaluate the damn thing."

Bailey frowned, but not because of anything to do with Gunney. She undid the screws, muttering curses about the bass-ackwards way her Toyota Tundra was constructed since getting at the screws with any tool was absurdly difficult. Then they lifted the plastic covering and examined her air filter.

It was mostly white—not pristine, but still in pretty good shape.

"That clears *that* up," the old mechanic commented. "Unscrewing the fucking cover was probably more trouble than it was worth."

The girl gritted her teeth. Gunney noticed.

"What's wrong?" he asked. "Something I said?"

"Yeah," she admitted, "but not your fault. What you said... Goddammit. It's like *exactly* what's going on with this council bullshit."

He cocked an eyebrow, curious. "Oh? How so? Usually I'm the one coming up with, uh, metaphors or allegories or whatever the English Literature majors call them. You're moving up in the world if you don't need me to make them for you."

She snickered at that and pulled her torso away from the guts of the truck, standing up straight. "More trouble than it's worth to evaluate something. In this case, me. These all-powerful, all-knowing deities think I'm important enough to throw me through all this crap. I don't know what they have in mind, but once again, it's because they think I'm 'dangerous.' I've never been dangerous except to assholes who don't know to leave me alone. Have I?"

Gunney shrugged. "You always liked fighting," he pointed out, "but you never *picked* a fight with someone who hadn't done shit. Not that I heard of, anyway. Some people think anyone's a threat if they don't kiss ass and bend over backwards for them. Maybe some gods are the same way."

She grimaced. "I'm just so tired of being judged. I accept that I have more responsibilities now, but mostly I'd like to spend my time fixing cars, driving around with Roland, drinking beer, and watching the sunset, y'know?"

"I do," he replied. "Believe me. But like you told me, you've gone through all the motions, obeying their requests, doing everything you're supposed to, and they're *still* suspicious. At that point, the problem is on their end, not yours."

She took the rag from him and wiped her hands off, then closed the Tundra's hood. "Yeah, but it's harder to ignore someone else's problem when they're a frickin' deity."

"Well," Gunney continued, "you're one too, aren't you? I say maybe it's time you stood up and judged *them*. Don't budge on your beliefs. Stick to your story—which is true— and call them as you see them. If nothing else, they'll have to respect your honesty, and that can get you far. Respect and the knowledge that a person doesn't go around saying what people think they want to hear."

She took a deep breath and gave the old man a hug before accepting the keys back from him. "I think you're right. Thanks, Gunney. And I promise when this is over, I'll be back in the shop to help more often. One of these days, Fenris will stop dragging me into interdimensional adventures and all that crap."

Bailey said her goodbyes and drove the truck away from the auto shop through the darkened, sleepy town before arriving back in her own front yard. She felt a little better. Both her mentors believed in her, and her brothers backed her up.

She still missed Roland. As she lay down in her own room on her own bed for the first time in what felt like far too long, she wished he was next to her, kissing her cheek as they traded sarcastic comments and stroked each other's hair.

"Soon," she breathed and fell asleep.

CHAPTER FOURTEEN

The chamber was in the same extradimensional palace as the council chamber and the crystal hallway that led up to it, though it was not accessible from either. All six of the deities who sat in the bright chamber on their thrones had quarters here, and only those few who knew the necessary secrets could gain entry.

The doorway before the chamber was crafted of dark bronze. Engraved in its center was a crudely drawn smirking face, one replicated on the relic mortal men called the Snaptun Stone.

Fenris reached out and pushed open the door, then stepped into the quarters beyond.

The decor was paradoxical; the whole space was dark to the point of being cavernous, yet it was appointed with hangings, furniture, art, and plants in a riotous clash of bright, even obnoxious colors, most of which went poorly together.

Loki always said he considered it a joke.

Fenris approached the desk where the trickster god sat reading a book. "Hello, father," he intoned.

Loki snapped the book shut with a twist of his fingers and flung it over his shoulder. It flapped and squawked like a bird before finding its way to its place on the shelf, albeit upside down.

"Fenris," he responded. He stretched his long, thin limbs. "I expected you to show up, of course, and part of me was hoping for it. Does that make sense? I expect not." He tittered as though revisiting a private jest.

The wolf-god took four heavy steps closer. He did not speak.

Loki's dark eyes flickered with something no other being could comprehend: a unique form of madness. Insanity that enjoyed itself and would reject every opportunity to be cured. It had marinated and percolated over the eons, not giving in to reason or sense.

The thin man steepled his fingers. "I know how things might very well play out, you know. And I wonder," he sighed, "if it might be a good bit of *fun*."

Fenris continued his slow, inexorable approach. He was three steps from the desk. "What do you think is going to happen?"

The narrow, twisted smile on Loki's mouth widened. "Simply put, *disaster*. A disaster of the greatest, most magnificent kind. Something remarkable, noteworthy. *History*-worthy."

Fenris said nothing in response, only made a brief growling sound in his throat to indicate that he'd heard.

Loki went on, looking at his fireplace and tapping his lips with a bony finger. "I suspect, of course, that you're here to kill me. To remove the one unpredictable element from the coming situation—that nonsense with the vote. The others are predictable. Including Coyote, who's supposed to be a trickster too, but he has nothing on me. I'm known for being rather more mischievous. Not that I was around much during your initial existence, since fatherhood never suited me, but you know me well. You know that I might, if the fancy struck me, do something rash and crazed."

Fenris took another step.

"Something," Loki almost sneered, "that would disrupt your plans."

"And what," the wolf-deity queried, "do you think my plans are?"

His father laughed. "Not think, *know*. I know you plan to start Ragnarök exactly as the prophecy says! You're predictable too, at the end of the day. I'm nearly certain how you plan to do it."

Fenris did not react in any obvious fashion, save that his right hand balled into a fist.

"Yet," Loki rambled, "you can only achieve that if you remain on your current path, which means that you need that lovely girl Bailey for some bizarre reason. Therefore," he smacked the desk's surface for emphasis, "there remains the possibility that I might ply my wily ways and vote in a fashion that could make this little referendum *terribly* difficult for you."

Fenris stopped. His knees were brushing the far end of the desk. Only three feet of wood separated him from the god who'd sired him.

"Correct," he proclaimed, then paused. "I would apologize for what I am about to do, but that would be insincere. Besides," a small smile, as twisted as his father's, creased his face, "I imagine you find this all mildly amusing. Don't you?"

"Of course I do," Loki confirmed. He stood up in a deliberate and unhurried way, then spread his skinny arms in a wide gesture, basking in the moment. "But take care, Fenris, my son. I am not a being easily outmaneuvered, let alone destroyed. In fact, I've considered that—"

The attack came without warning. A huge dark shape, no longer human, was no longer standing on the other side of the desk but had stormed over it. The figures rolled amidst the bookcases, knocking two over. Wood and leather and bodies crashed to the floor.

A cacophony of horrible noises filled the chamber, howls and snarls, screams and whooshes, the sounds of terrible impacts, liquids striking the marble tiles, wood splintering, and flesh tearing beneath the impact of overwhelming force and millennia of pent-up hatred.

The flickering flames of the stone fireplace cast the struggle in jagged black shadows on the wall and in front of it as silhouettes, the two forms indistinguishable in their frenzied violence.

Then it was over. Only one black shape moved.

The form shuffled past the fire, its outline unrecognizable as anything human, sane, or sensible, possibly covered with fur, but an observer would have had difficulty being sure. It changed as it moved, growing slimmer and more definitely human.

Beyond the fireplace was a great mirror lined with burnished gold. The figure examined his reflection.

Though his skin and bones still rippled in places, his form was stabilizing—a thin, dark-haired man wearing an enigmatic smile. Incongruously, he also wore a big, bulky, hooded coat.

The man frowned and the coat shifted, becoming a perfect replica of the sleek, dark suit the man at the desk had worn. He nodded in satisfaction.

"Bailey," he whispered to himself, "we're done here. Now it's on you."

The girl hugged her brothers, who stood in a line on the back porch to see her off. The morning was bright and pleasant; part of her regretted she couldn't spend another day, or another week, enjoying the weather and doing normal stuff around town.

But the challenge that lay before her wouldn't go away simply because she felt like procrastinating. She intended to deal with it before it loomed too large, then move on with her life.

Jacob held her gaze. "Be careful. I know we always say obvious shit like that, but it's kinda required."

She flashed them a rueful smile. "You know I don't mind. I'll be fine."

Turning away, she raised her arms and called, "*Fenris!*" imbuing her voice with magic that rippled through the fabric of multiple dimensions. He might have heard her normal voice if he was listening, but she'd rather be thorough about it. She listened to the echo as it reverberated within the Hearth Valley and crept up into the mountains.

It took less than a minute. A doorway of glowing amethyst-hued liquid opened before her and out stepped her god and teacher.

"Are you ready?" he asked.

"Yup," she affirmed. "I'm nice and rested and all that. I think it's time to get this over with."

He nodded and waved her toward the portal. "Good. Come along."

Raising her hand to her brothers, she stepped through, with Fenris following her.

Once more they emerged in the glittering crystal hallway, which stretched for what looked like a mile toward a haze-covered arch. Before they started toward their destination, Fenris put a hand on the werewitch's shoulder.

"I must leave," he told her. "I can't say why, but I'm not able to be present during the trial. You will do fine, however. Do what they say, believe in yourself, and remember all you've learned thus far."

Suddenly, in a delayed reaction that was stronger than it should have been *because* of the delay, the girl was afraid. She'd faced up to what was coming and was confident she could handle it.

But she'd envisioned Fenris being there for her. She'd never seen herself as having to face down half a dozen gods alone.

No, she insisted, and her will rose up to blot out her fear. *We're doing this. He'll be with me in spirit whether he's standing there or not. He's said time and again that I have what it takes.*

Bailey strode down the hall. When she looked back over her shoulder a moment later, Fenris was gone. So was the portal they'd come through. She briefly wondered if the wolf-father had headed back to Earth or somewhere else.

It didn't matter. Only what lay ahead was important.

Nearing the arch, however, she realized she might not be alone after all. A familiar figure, tall, dark, and muscular, stood before the opening.

"Carl," she marveled. "How the hell did you get here?"

He smiled. "I'm Balder's pupil, remember? And half-god myself. I figured you could use someone like me to vouch for you. I was sent to spy on you, so now's my chance to deliver my report about how you're an insane terrorist who should be destroyed immediately."

She snorted and punched him in the arm. "Ha-ha. Cute."

"Or something like that." He scratched his head. "Whatever I say, it will be the truth."

She breathed in, then out. "Can't ask for more than that."

In unison, they stepped through the incandescent fog that separated the corridor from the chamber, and the heavens stretched before them beyond the crystal windows.

The six chairs were empty. Bailey's brow furrowed and she spun, glancing everywhere at once, mentally and physically shifting into combat mode in case something was wrong.

Carl was less alarmed but still concerned. "This is odd," he remarked. "Wait, here they come. We got here early, is all."

Her sextet of judges strode through the hazy barrier.

Bailey wondered why she and Carl hadn't seen them in the hall, and it occurred to her that the arch might be a portal, with each deity approaching from a different place.

Freya was there, resplendent in silver and green, haughtily ignoring her. Balder's face was cast in its customary enigmatic neutrality, and there was the boisterous bluster of Thor, the solemn wisdom of Thoth, the good-natured humor of Coyote. Last to arrive was Loki, who wore a disquieting little smirk.

The six took their seats and nodded at Bailey.

Freya looked around. "How odd," she announced, "that Fenris chose not to be here to see his apprentice perform."

Loki chuckled, steepling his fingers. "Perhaps," he posited, "the old wolf-god is afraid of what the outcome might be, and like a dog smelling a bear, tucked tail and ran off, content to bark from the ridge until someone gives him a treat for being so bold."

Low laughter went around the semicircle of the seated gods. Coyote did not participate for obvious reasons, but the rest seemed amused by the joke at Fenris's expense.

Bailey fumed, and her right hand balled into a fist. As far as she was concerned, the session was off on the wrong foot. It strengthened her desire to prove them all wrong.

Beside her, she felt Carl's presence. A subtle vibe emanated from him, urging her to control her anger. To save it for later and use it when the time was right rather than wasting it. She calmed down and waited for the referendum to begin.

Thoth spread his hands.

"Let us hesitate no longer. Bailey Nordin, you are here today in part because one of our members made a poor choice. It stemmed from our broader concerns about you and the role you will play in our universe. Since the first manifestation of your powers, chaos and destruction have followed you everywhere. There are many who believe you to be an ill-disciplined agent of violence and disorder. One who may, furthermore, be suffused with dangerous levels of ego and ambition. How do you answer these charges?"

In her opinion, they'd been over this before, but she went through the motions anyway in the hope that it demonstrated her patience and regaled them with the whole story. She filled in details of everything that had happened since Freya had first appeared to her and Roland months ago.

She explained that she had agreed to the council's suggestion that she go to the training grounds, and elaborated upon having met Carl and Ragnar and worked with the scion to save as many people as she could from Ragnar's rampage. She'd remained at the grounds for further study until Fenris summoned her before the six deities.

Heads turned and the gods all looked at one another, exchanging subtle nods and gestures. They looked back at the young woman before them.

"We agree," Thoth said, "that you seem to possess greater control than you had when you were first brought before us. The difference is not as pronounced as we would like, but the fact remains that you have shown improvement in a very short time."

The girl blinked. She'd expected them to throw another bullshit accusation or challenge her way. Instead, they'd complimented her.

"Uh, thanks," she stammered. "I try. And I usually succeed."

Thoth went on before she could comment further. "However, this by itself is not enough. We must know more about your abilities, your judgment, and your temperament. Each of us has specific concerns of his or her own. Thus, in order to proceed, you must pass a series of tests put to you by every member of this council."

Bailey tried not to grimace. *Fuck. Nothing can ever be easy, can it? Well, Fenris told me they'd require this.*

The six stood up from their seats, continuing to stare straight at her, then five of them turned and filed to the sides of the chamber, circling its periphery before making their way out through the hazy barrier. None objected to the presence of Carl, who had remained standing near the far corner of the chamber.

The deity who remained was Balder. Rather than follow his brethren, he took two steps forward, his bright blue eyes staring into Bailey's while his beautiful face became somehow grimmer and more severe.

"Good day, Bailey," he began. "I will be the first to challenge you, a simple test. *Combat.* Not to the death, merely an assessment of your skill as a melee fighter. Have you a preferred weapon?"

Bailey wondered if she could trust a god to play fair in a duel. She didn't think he intended for her to beat him, simply make a good showing.

"Short swords," she suggested. "Two of them, if possible, or one short sword and a buckler?"

Balder smiled. "Done. Look behind you."

She turned, and floating in midair was a blade much

like the ones she'd used at the training grounds, something halfway between a Roman gladius and a Viking-era sword, though much finer. Its hilt was worked with gold and diamonds, and the blade was so polished it could double as a mirror.

Next to it was a small handheld shield that looked like it was made of solid silver, though it must have been a harder and stronger metal that was enchanted or overlaid.

Bailey took both items in her hands and turned back to the god of light and beauty, who had drawn his own sword and raised his own shield. They were similar to hers but slightly larger, and his shield was gold rather than silver.

Behind her, she saw Carl tense as he watched the pair fall into a fighting stance.

The deity raised his golden shield toward the girl, his sword held high behind him. "On your guard, Bailey Nordin. Begin!"

She brought up her buckler in time to intercept Balder's stunningly fast sword stroke. The shining blade slid off the curved surface, but the force behind the blow was enough to drive her back a step.

Balder pressed his advantage, as she'd figured he would. She moved her buckler in a small circle before her, the better to ward off blows from multiple directions, and two strong hits sent shockwaves up her arm. At the same time, she ducked down and forward, swiping her own sword at Balder's legs.

She did no real damage, but one stroke to his knee gave him enough pause for her to shove her shield into his side while stabbing at his face. She knew he'd avoid it; the goal was to distract and imbalance him.

For a moment, it seemed she'd succeed. Then the god rallied and pressed her with stunning speed and power. It was all she could do to keep her shield in front of her face or torso while relying on her were agility to protect her limbs.

Then her sword came down on Balder's arm an inch or two above the elbow; the wound was not severe, but on a mortal, it would have drawn blood. He bled shining golden ichor instead.

Balder's sword lunged out in retaliation and grazed the girl's hip as she pivoted away, leaving a cut in her pants and scratching the skin. The combatants separated, eyeing each other.

Surprisingly, the tall god smiled and sheathed his sword. "We are done," he stated. "I could have fought harder had I wished to vanquish you, but I did not go easy on you either, and you made a good showing."

"Thanks," she panted. The blade and buckler vanished from her hands.

"You seem more in control," the blond deity added, "more measured and tactics-minded. And though it may not have been obvious to you previously, you were bleeding excess magic when you came before us the first time. You have gained control over the worst of that."

Indeed, she hadn't known, but now that she'd learned more, she believed it.

Balder went on, "Carl has told me good things about you. Between that and your fine performance here today, I believe you deserve a chance. Carl? Do you still feel the same way?"

The dark-skinned scion stepped forward and gestured at the girl as she stood catching her breath.

"Yes, my lord. Bailey has done well, and I've no reason to suspect her motivations or question her integrity. I agree with your decision."

Balder smiled at the girl. "You have my 'yea' vote, Bailey Nordin." He stepped back, then strode toward the arch.

The werewitch called after him, "Vote for what?" He did not respond and vanished behind the screen of effervescent mist.

Clemency, she supposed, but beyond that, she had no understanding of the significance of yea versus nay.

Before she could ponder the matter further, in stomped Thor Odinson.

"Bailey!" he roared. "It is my turn. I've come to test you with Mjölnir. Are you ready?"

With that, he pulled his hammer out of thin air. Mounted on a short handle, its double-sided head looked especially mighty and incredibly heavy. She could not say what material it was made of, possibly a strange amalgamation of stone, steel, and perhaps platinum.

She drew herself up to her full height. "Do I get a weapon too?"

The god laughed. "No, we're not fighting. Mjölnir is a weapon, but it's more than that. It has always been used to test the mettle of those who might wield it. As a youth, I was self-centered, impetuous, and foolish. I had to improve before I could lift the hammer. We shall see if you require similar refinement."

With a flippant motion, he tossed the hammer in front

of him. It moved in a short arc and then fell to the floor with a heavy clank, head down, the haft sticking upwards.

Thor raised a finger. "To clarify, the test is not to see if you are like me. None are! Rather, it is to determine if you have the self-control any god must possess."

He lowered his voice for the first time, speaking little above a whisper. "Can you put your duties above your personal desires, Bailey Nordin? Can you enforce the discipline you'll need to do the right thing?"

The girl looked at the hammer that rested two paces in front of her. She stepped forward and made ready to kneel, staring at it. It didn't look *that* heavy up close.

Yet, something about the way it had landed as if someone had dropped a two-ton anvil on a powerful magnet...

She wrapped her hands around the hilt and waited for something to happen. Nothing did.

Am I doing something wrong? Shit. Think about what Thor said, Bailey. Duty. Self-control. That's what's important.

She reflected on all Fenris had shown her, the responsibilities of shamanhood and godhood, and the people back home depending on her.

Bailey lifted, and the hammer rose in her hands. It felt like it weighed perhaps three pounds. Her eyes widened in shock.

Thor clapped a hand to his belly. "Ha! Ha, ha, oh, that's rich! What do you plan to do with it now?" He looked at her askance, one eye staring into hers beneath its bushy red brow.

Raising the hammer, she found that it didn't seem all

that powerful. It wasn't much different from a basic mallet she might have used in Gunney's shop.

She shrugged and handed it back to Thor. "It's yours, not mine," she said. "But I passed, didn't I?"

"Indeed!" The thunder god put the weapon behind his back, and it vanished into thin air. "Mjölnir would not have served you or empowered you the way it does me, for it is bound to me alone, yet its ability to refuse to be picked up by the unworthy applies to all. Well done."

With a respectful jerk of his wide chin, Thor left.

Bailey sighed and exchanged satisfied glances with Carl, who'd continued to watch from his corner. Before they could speak, the shimmering barrier parted again, and in came Coyote.

"Why, hello," the trickster greeted her, pawing one of his ears. "You seem sharp. Perceptive. But not everyone, or everything, is as they seem. Let us test the true extent of your capabilities."

Something shimmered and wavered. The girl couldn't see what was happening for a second or two, then suddenly, a dozen Coyotes stood before her. Their movements were perfectly synchronized, and when the deity spoke, she couldn't tell which one the sound came from. It may have been that all spoke simultaneously, the sound blended into a single voice.

"You may point only once," Coyote explained. "Observe, and point at the one of us who is real. The others are but illusions. Choose wisely, Bailey."

Crap, she cursed. *This is like that thing in the temple with the two statues, but they at least gave us riddles, and we had the signs to go by, too. No hints this time, and if there was a way to tell where the real Coyote was as he conjured the others, I missed it.*

Sweat stood out on her brow, and her stomach fluttered. Then she thought of something.

Closing her eyes, she created an illusion of herself, then doubled it as Deona the trainer had taught her, and further doubled the doubles until she had sixteen plus her original self; more than Coyote's twelve. She dismissed the four "extra" ones.

The werewitch spent a moment synchronizing the clones' movements to her own. When she was confident they'd act in flawless unison, she had them line up in front of the dozen Coyotes.

Then all of them pointed at the figure in front of them. Once.

The doglike figures all let out short, barking, yipping laughs, and eleven of them vanished, leaving one two spaces to Bailey's right as the real deity.

"Clever!" he admitted and kept chuckling. "Technically, you are correct since you did point only once, and you did point at the real me. Your solution rivals the best of my jokes, and it demonstrates a mastery of that flexibility of thinking we require to power through situations when the rules seem to make things all but impossible."

He gave her a gentle squeeze on the shoulder as she stood, trying not to grin too blatantly, then ambled out of the chamber.

Thoth was next. He did nothing save stand before her, his tall, dark form imposing but not malicious. He reminded her of the principal of her elementary school, whom she'd been sent to a couple times after misbehaving.

The silence between them dragged out until the girl felt like shouting at him just to break it.

Then he did. "What, Bailey Nordin," the Egyptian god of wisdom queried, "do you intend to do as a goddess?" He fell silent and waited.

The werewitch had to admit she was pretty much baffled by the question.

"I'm not sure," she confessed. "Watch over things, help my people, and take care of them. Beyond that, I don't know; I'll deal with it as I come to it. I'm willing to listen to the council's advice. Doesn't mean I'll blindly do whatever you say since I can make judgments of my own, but I'll consider your expert opinions before I jump to any conclusions."

Thoth did not respond or react in any way. It appeared that he wanted more out of her.

"Honestly," she went on, "all I ever wanted was to have at least a little freedom to myself, but otherwise, for all the people I care about to be happy and safe. I'd use my powers to help the people I'm responsible for, but I'd be smart about it. I'd listen to the rest of you on how best to do that without messing things up."

The eyes of the deity rolled slightly back in his head, and she perceived that he was contemplating her words.

His broad mouth spread into something that came close to a smile, though not quite. "Very well," he stated. "Wisdom, magic, and truth are part of my mantle, and I detect no lie in your answer, which is sound and will suffice. You shall move on."

She sighed. "Good."

With no further words, Thoth turned and left.

The instant he stepped through the barrier in one direction, Loki passed him from the other. The Norse god of mischief, his black hair trailing behind him in the air, did not stop or alter his pace, but walked straight toward the girl, halting a single step in front of her.

"Hmm," he said, looking her over. "Eh. She's fine. No test." He gave her a wink, smirked with amusement, and turned to go.

Bailey stood blinking, and Carl came up beside her. "He probably thinks it's funny," he mentioned. "Undermining how seriously the other gods are taking this. But it means you got another 'yea' vote."

She shrugged. "I'll take what I can get."

Loki's departure left only one more deity.

In came Freya, moving with a slow, swaying gait, faintly ethereal while seeming real and earthy in her subdued haughtiness. The greenish light that hovered around her head resembled the glow of lightning in distant storm clouds.

"You," the goddess proclaimed, pointing a finger at Bailey's face, "are a loose cannon. You are guilty of malevolence through ineptitude. Your inability to control your powers or grasp your place in the greater scheme of things has led to more problems and more suffering than you purport to have resolved. Answer this charge!"

Rage boiled up in Bailey. She knew better than to give in to it; she also knew how to use it as fuel for her resolve.

"No one else seems to think that," she pointed out, her face neutral but her jaw firmly set, "and it sounds an awful lot like you're accusing me of what you yourself are guilty of to deflect blame and suspicion. Ragnar killed a dozen innocent people before he tried to take me out. How is that my fault? How can you expect to sit on this council, judging me, when you didn't make a good decision about who to send to keep an eye on me?"

Freya's eyes widened, and her face fell as though someone had spat on her. Bailey had seen the look on mortals; it was no different on a goddess. It was the way someone's face appeared when they were about to lash out.

"You dare?" the lady of witchcraft rasped. "You dare arrogate the right to question my competence? I, who have watched over humankind for eons?"

Her hands leapt up, crackling with the combined powers of every element of both magic and nature. She was going to strike.

There was a flash of light, but not from the goddess. Five forms phased into sight, materializing directly into their chairs. The other gods had returned to the chamber to head off the confrontation.

"Freya," Thoth boomed, "that is enough. You would kill her on our floor out of a sense of personal grievance? That would be most reckless."

Fuming, the goddess let the power in her grasp fade and choked back whatever comment she was preparing to blurt.

The Egyptian raised his hand and announced, "We shall hear last testaments from all present before taking our final vote. Then it shall be decided who sits in that chair."

When he gestured at the empty seat, Bailey and Freya did nothing but stare each other down.

"We've heard enough," said Thoth. "Let the vote proper commence."

The Oregonian werewitch and the Norse patron of sorcery stood side by side, the newer goddess and the old, and waited for the pronouncement. Each deity including Freya had submitted their personal commentary and the results of their tests. Carl had also stepped in to defend Bailey, and she'd been given one final opportunity to defend herself as well.

As the girl waited, she could feel the storm of agitation growing in the powerful entity to her left. Freya was not like Aradia; she was stronger, but also more emotional and elemental. Both of them knew the information favored Bailey's side of the story.

Thoth looked around, and something invisible passed between him and the other four who sat on their thrones. Finally, he looked at Freya, who did not return his gaze.

The Egyptian spread his hands. "So be it. By a vote of five to one, this council finds Freya unfit to fulfill her role at present and agrees to give Bailey a chance to sit in the vacant chair. Perhaps the best test for her is to perform those duties until Freya's better judgment returns."

Bailey closed her eyes as relief surged through her.

"What? This is farcical! Absurd!" Freya ranted. "She was a mortal mere months ago! This is unprecedented. I demand redress!"

Thor scoffed. "Redress? You agreed to abide by the council's decision!"

Coyote shook his head. "I'm afraid that's true, Freya. You cannot treat the vote as illegitimate when we all supported it as a means of decision. And you will be allowed to return to the council in time. Perhaps you might enjoy leaving behind the burden of its responsibilities?"

The goddess did not reply to the thunder-god or the jokester, just spun to face Bailey.

"I challenge her to combat by magic. If she would sit among us, let her prove she is as strong as we are in a duel to the death!"

The girl returned the Norse deity's blazing stare. She was cold inside, though, not only due to the danger involved in dueling another divine being—one more powerful than she'd faced before—but because of the uncanny sense that Fenris had *known* this would happen.

Had he? she wondered. *Was he preparing me not for a possibility but for a certainty? Did he try to act like it might not happen to bolster my courage or avoid the implications that he was sending me directly against his sister? In any event, he sure as shit did the right thing by training me for it.*

Murmurs, glances, and gestures were exchanged by the

five seated deities as they discussed the prospect of permitting a one-on-one battle between the contending pair.

Thor made a grumbling sound. "I like it not. It is the old way of doing things, well-established and better than plotting behind someone's back, yes, but much could go wrong. Yet, if Freya will not accept our judgment, we may have no choice."

Balder frowned, and Loki wore no expression.

Coyote offered his two cents. "The duel need not be to the death."

Freya snapped at him, "They are always to the death. For something of this magnitude, it must be."

Sighing, Thoth waved a hand and said, "Very well, Freya. You shall be given this one last chance to have your own way. But take care; you yourself have insisted that the loser be destroyed. Aradia underestimated Bailey and paid the ultimate price for it."

The girl's mind raced with random thoughts she tried to keep quiet, replacing them with all that she'd learned about magical battles, including Fenris's most recent lessons. Wards. Deflector shields. Advanced grounding of divine beings.

The other gods directed the combatants to stand at opposite sides of the chamber, their backs to the walls, facing each other. Meanwhile, the seated five collaborated on a powerful shield that walled them off from the pyrotechnics to come.

Thoth raised his hand, then lowered it in a chopping motion. "Begin."

Bailey instantly surrounded her own body with a thick shield, rippled and with a deflective surface, and conjured a ward to protect her against electricity. Lightning seemed to be Freya's favorite elemental attack.

She realized how good an idea this was when a storm of green thunderbolts converged on her from multiple directions. Freya advanced slowly, her hands raised and crackling with power.

The werewitch could barely see. Though her ward kept her safe from the lightning, it created an enormous amount of visual interference. She conjured another pair of deflective shields ahead of her and off to the sides, then seized control of three of Freya's bolts.

One she sent straight ahead at the goddess. The other two she tossed at angles, so they ricocheted off the shields before streaking toward Freya's flanks.

The goddess seemed surprised by the tactic, but she blocked or neutralized the bolts with ease and took another step forward, summoning a gale-force windstorm laden with sharp fragments of diamond and steel.

Bailey tried to push forward, using a thick shield in front of her to block and reflect the onslaught, but there was too much of it—too much raw power. She summoned another ward to guard her against kinetic impact, which she hoped would work for both blasts of concussive force and the blows of flying solid objects.

Freya advanced, arms undulating as she summoned strange animal specters to lunge at Bailey while surgically precise blades of arcanoplasm began to carve apart her shields, opening gaps through which a killing strike could be delivered.

For a moment, the girl despaired. Fighting Freya was like struggling against the wrath of nature as directed by a witch with more knowledge and experience than she could fathom.

Bailey tried opening the necessary channel to ground and drain the goddess, but she could not get through the constant magical assaults. Soon, Freya would overwhelm her.

"God*dammit!*" she grated, wracking her brain and bolstering her courage. She remembered her four-way duel with Carl.

A duplicate image of herself appeared right on top of her to disguise which one was real, then she and the illusion stepped in opposite directions behind the fragmenting shield. She doubled and quadrupled the illusion, and as she started conjuring a new shield, her clones did likewise.

Freya pressed ahead, filling the air with a chaos of elements combined with subtle psionic efforts to weaken her opponent, but now the goddess strove against five enemies instead of one. Bailey directed two of her doubles to begin attacking the goddess with looping arcs of lightning, horizontal waves of plasma, and whirlwinds of ice and fire.

Freya paused, needing an instant to grasp the nature of the changes in the battle, and it gave Bailey enough time. Barely enough.

She imagined once again a tendril emerging from her forehead to shoot out and plant itself in Freya's heart. At the same time, she envisioned roots growing from her legs into the ground, connecting her to the substance of the divine realm, which would absorb bled-off magical energy like a giant sponge beneath a leaky faucet.

The lady of witchcraft gasped audibly, and the greenish

light of her eyes wavered as the tendril struck true. She knew what was happening.

"No," Freya raged. "You will not do to me what you did to Aradia! I'm many times stronger than she was, and not constrained by the pact."

Bailey could feel the goddess' incredible power flowing out and through her, noticing she absorbed some of it herself. The store of it was so vast that it would take time to weaken her to the point of destruction.

Freya still had plenty of time in which to kill her.

Pressurized lances of poisoned water and acid sprouted from the goddess, moving slowly at first, then increasing their speed as they advanced, their courses irregular and impossible to predict. The shields blocked most of them, but Bailey was unable to maintain enough mental control over one of her illusions to have it repair its barrier in time, and the deadly projectiles blasted the double into fading fragments of light.

The ground beneath Bailey's feet melted, turning to boiling liquid, but she blocked the heat and conjured a sheet of crystal below her, jumping up to land on it just as it came into existence. Her clones did likewise, one of them continuing to harry Freya with meteor-like fireballs.

The five other gods watched the battle with intense expressions, but none spoke or intervened.

Bailey felt as though every nerve and synapse were on fire and supercharged with caffeine. The arcane might of the rival goddess was nearly impossible to channel without panicking at the magnitude of it, but she'd done this before. The process was the same as with Aradia, only more so, and her clones were automated well enough to provide limited cover and protection.

Still, if Freya didn't weaken soon...

The goddess went to one knee, the indignity of it contrasting with her beauty and haughty demeanor, and the strength of her attacks ebbed.

Behind their protective wall, the quintet began discussing what they watched.

"Incredible," Balder remarked, "to see Freya unleash the full force of her abilities. Bailey has demonstrated impressive control to have resisted her."

"Aye," Thor agreed. "And she's grounded her! An ugly sight, but we all knew it might happen."

"Clever," said Coyote. "Bailey can't match her in raw strength, which has pushed her to use her skills in innovative ways."

Thoth stroked his chin. "There are wisdom and recklessness on both sides, but sometimes, both are needed."

Loki said nothing. He leaned forward, however, watching the duel with gleeful interest and paying particular attention to the way Bailey grew stronger as Freya grew weaker.

The power of another goddess would soon be hers.

The two combatants had taken to roaring and screaming, trying to intimidate the other with primitive rage despite the careful control they imposed on their complex magical attacks and defenses. Freya conjured two clones of her own to help her, but Bailey directed her doubles to shift into wolf form, tackle them, and destroy them.

And the tide turned. Freya stumbled back, face drawn and pale, on a defensive footing now as Bailey assaulted her with increasingly massive blasts of magic. All the while, the werewitch bled her essence to power her own spells or dissipated it into the fabric of the universe.

"No," Freya said again, but this time it was a pleading gasp. "No, this cannot happen!"

Bailey stomped forward, battering aside the goddess's weakening attacks. The portion of Freya's magic she'd absorbed had replenished her stamina, and she felt like she could crush Freya underfoot like a bug.

The goddess fell onto her hands and knees, looking less like a deity than like a simple mortal woman who'd lost the strength to resist anything.

Bailey stopped. Rage boiled within her; anger at the supercilious nastiness of the gods and Freya in particular, exasperation at the unnecessary conflicts and all the hoops she'd had to jump through. Part of her wanted to snuff the goddess out and make an example of her.

But what kind of example would that set?

The girl drew in a breath and dispelled her illusions and storming attacks. She kept her shields up in case Freya tried a last-ditch attack, but she stopped fighting.

"I win," Bailey stated. "I could destroy you if I wanted to. The rules would allow it. But I'd rather not. Instead..." She thought of something, "It might be best if you teach me what I need to know as a witch-goddess, like how Fenris is showing me how to minister to wolves. Show me what it takes to sit in your chair, if only for a while."

Freya's luminous eyes widened as her mouth slowly fell open. The anger and hostility seemed to be melting away from her. She was shocked, but not in a bad way.

Thoth stood up from his throne. "It is done. Bailey won

the duel, and has chosen to spare Freya, meaning that she will, as previously agreed, have the opportunity to return to her seat on this council when the time is right."

The other gods stood, joining the Egyptian, and the next to speak was Balder.

"Bailey," he said in his soft voice, "thank you for allowing my sister to live. We were confident in your growing wisdom and talent. Now we are confident in your compassion and mercy as well."

Thor grunted with approval. "Yes. 'Tis true that by rights, you could have killed her under the formal rules of a mortal duel, yet you chose the higher-handed way of doing things. I'd rather not lose her either, even if at times she needs to cool her head."

Coyote concurred. "The point was made; destroying Freya would have served no purpose, only left a great wound in the cosmos where she'd been. There is much she can teach the werewitch. This will be best for us all."

The only deity who declined to comment was Loki. He sat in calm, collected silence, his palms held together before him, smiling a faint smile that was rich with secret amusements.

Bailey wiped her brow, and as she brushed away the sweat, it was as though she were casting off the worst of the fears and anxieties she'd built up through the ordeal. She'd somehow known that the peace and security she'd purchased by defeating Aradia wouldn't last and a new challenge would emerge. Winning over half a dozen ancient gods was something she'd by no means been certain about.

Despite being a goddess.

Freya climbed to her feet; she seemed weak and tired. "I," she breathed, pausing, "accept this outcome. Perhaps I judged you too harshly, Bailey Nordin. I should have been more careful and thoughtful. I own up to that. For now, I offer you my seat on the council, and I will give you my advice if you'll have it."

"I will." Bailey smiled. "Thank you, and I'm glad things turned out the way they did."

The seven figures stood in a circle then and clasped hands to seal the deal. Everyone agreed to immediately conduct the rite that would welcome Bailey onto the council.

Thoth smiled with surprising warmth. "The initiation ceremony is less intense than you might think," he explained, "though you should find it satisfactory. The idea is to remind the initiate of the importance of her responsibilities rather than to dazzle her with her importance, you see."

Bailey nodded. "Yeah, makes sense. I won't lie; I'm happy I've made it this far. But Fenris taught me well, and I know that this is about other people and the good of the world, not about me getting the chance to strut in front of everyone."

A jeweled chest appeared, and Balder opened it and took out golden scepters, which he passed out to almost everyone. Bailey did not get one, but Thoth got two. The five who sat on the council lined up before their seats and spoke of their long vigil over the world and its inhabitants, and their mission to ensure that wisdom prevailed throughout all the spheres of existence.

Freya stood aside and watched, pained but accepting, as

Bailey stepped forward and accepted one of the scepters from Thoth.

The Egyptian god stated, "Sit in your place and know that your duties are only beginning. You have our trust, but also the burden of our expectations."

She sat in the chair. "I understand."

The seat was comfortable. Looking out across the chamber, she felt no different, really. She was pretty sure she could get used to this.

Freya sat in the great chair of roots and vines, perfectly grown to accommodate her lithe shape, which dominated her personal quarters adjacent to the main council room. The entire chamber resembled a large and elaborate cottage, or perhaps a temple built into the base of a tree in a dense northern forest.

Yet it was clean and orderly and decorated with a variety of arcane artifacts. Green and brown and silver predominated. A subtle sound wafted on the air, like that of a breeze moving between leaves, with the occasional rustle of wooden wind chimes. There was no fireplace, but weather magic kept the temperature on the cusp between cool and warm.

The goddess leaned forward, her face in her hands, her silver-green dress torn and dirtied by the fight against the girl. Noticing this, she flicked a finger. The dress cleaned and repaired itself.

Four quick taps sounded on the door. "Who is that? Loki?" She doubted anyone else would knock that way.

The wooden portal swung inward. "Of course," her brother reassured her, stepping in nimbly on his long, lean legs, his black hair flapping back from his face.

Freya looked at him with a steady expression of mild distaste, mostly at having been disturbed.

"What are you doing here?" Her eyes flashed green with what remained of her sorcerous power. "And did you expect Bailey to triumph the way she did? You were curiously silent during the trials *and* the vote. And my duel against her."

Loki closed the door behind him and moved with light footwork deeper into the room, approaching the chair where the goddess rested.

"No," he admitted, "I had no idea how things would turn out. None of us, despite our knowledge and power, can predict the future with perfect accuracy. Any time we think we've done so, an unexpected variable arises and the whole course of the timeline shifts, taking us into uncharted territory before we can collate enough information to make another prediction."

The lady of witchcraft responded with a weary smile. "Of course. Such is the way of things. I could not have anticipated that the girl would win and then spare me. Perhaps she has potential worth developing, after all."

Loki nodded.

"But," Freya continued, "why have you come to speak to me? I would be a fool to assume it was to check on me or offer comfort. You always have a motive, albeit sometimes one that is incomprehensible to the rest of us."

Loki took a few more steps toward her. "Correct. I've

come because I cannot allow you to move in and begin counseling, training, and mentoring Bailey."

She sat up straight, alert, the mantle of weariness thrown from her and forgotten.

"What do you mean?" she snapped. "I may be off the council, but I am still a goddess. I have more right to advise her than Fenris does, certainly. What is your plan, Loki?"

He advanced one more step, then stopped. "To remove all potential opposition," he stated.

Freya's face went ashen as the fact of her weakened state struck her. It loomed between them, obvious in the face of an open threat. "You wanted me off the council, was that it? Well, you've succeeded. Now, leave! You have no reason to be here."

"Yes, I do," he replied. Then he changed.

Instead of the slim, compact man, smirking, smooth-faced, and black-haired, the figure before her was another, equally familiar. A taller, bulkier, and more grizzled man, with broad shoulders and a hood obscuring his craggy features.

Both gods cried out, speaking no words, only primal screams as magic crackled and the visitor pounced on his host.

Freya was greater in sorcery than Fenris, but Bailey had depleted her powers and left her weakened. The wolf-father's magic brushed hers aside, and his strong body, becoming bestial as he changed into his lupine form, crashed into hers. Wood splintered as the chair shattered, and the two deities tumbled to the floor.

The witch-goddess lay twisted and half-broken beneath

the bulk of her snarling brother, her eyes rolling in crazed terror and rage. Blood streamed down her face.

"I know what you're planning!" she shrieked, trying to claim a shred of triumph by flinging the accusation in his face. "Bastard! You mean to eliminate us all, to remove the safeguard we represent. To leave the doors open for Ragnarök. You fool!"

The huge wolf-monster grinned and drooled as he pressed down on her. "Yes," Fenris affirmed. "You are correct, except in thinking that I am a fool. Time will prove otherwise, but you will not be around to see it."

His jaws lashed out and snapped shut, the knife-like teeth shearing through flesh and bone.

Then the chamber fell silent. The beast heaved himself to his feet, already shifting back into the form of a tall man, and the hood of his coat regrew itself over his shaggy head.

He let out a long, shaky breath. "So it is done," he intoned. "You were never worthy to sit on the council, Freya. I will find some excuse for what's happened to you. The others have not yet missed Loki, and after all the trouble you caused with your pompousness and hotheaded choices, they will miss you even less."

Fenris turned away from the body of his sister and strode out of the room, allowing the wooden door to fall shut behind him.

Moments passed, and the sounds of the wolf-god's departure faded. The breeze and chimes were no more. Total quiet returned.

But not for long.

A dry, snickering laugh, low and sardonic, rose from the floor. The body it emanated from rose as well. It no longer resembled a woman, however. The inhabitant of the room had become a lean black-haired man.

"Nice try, Fenris," Loki whispered. He spread his hands, opened a portal of glimmering purple light, and stepped through it.

CHAPTER SIXTEEN

Someone knocked on the door.

Jacob rose from the couch. "I'll get it," he grumbled.

"Thanks," Kurt quipped. "I mean, it's not like you have anything intelligent to say when baseball is the only sport on TV, right? 'Oh, the guy swung and missed. He's going to strike out if he misses again. Yup.'"

"Don't make me...strike you out," Jacob muttered in a tired voice, then cursed.

Bailey squinted, and Russell leaned close to her. "Jacob was up late last night, trying to find out if anyone had heard from you. He's not his usual self."

"I guess not," his sister responded. "He didn't even throw anything at Kurt's head."

Behind and to the side of her, Fenris stood leaning against the wall. He'd reappeared a short while after Bailey had been inducted into the council and Thoth had explained the basics to her, saying that with the council's permission, it was time to go home.

No one had voiced any objections, least of all Bailey.

Jacob reached the front door and pulled it open.

"Hi," said Roland. "What'd I miss?"

Bailey looked up, biting down on a broad smile. "Everything. The hell were you off doing, anyway?"

The wizard snorted and stepped in, briefly greeting Jacob before joining the rest in the living room. "Everything. And you missed all of it."

She laughed, not feeling like maintaining the charade of teasing him. Instead, she stood up to wrap her arms around his neck. They exchanged a quick kiss, nothing too elaborate so as not to embarrass her brothers.

Rather than expound upon what he'd been up to, Roland asked how things had gone on Bailey's end. They snuggled together on the couch as she started to speak.

Though her brothers had heard the story at this point, they half-listened in between watching the game, though Russell left for a bit in the middle of it to make coffee and bring them all a steaming mug.

Roland, however, found his jaw hanging open for half the narrative. In the end, all he could do was shake his head slowly and rub his eyes.

"Astounding!" he exclaimed. "Inconceivable, almost, or some other pretentious adjective. Well, I'm glad you got through it and that they're also allowing you to come back home instead of having to sit on Mount Olympus or whatever it is all the time."

"Right," she agreed, unable to think of anything to add to that.

The wizard leaned back and folded his arms behind his head. "As for me, I was just, oh, you know, doing nothing.

Bored. Flirted with tons of other girls mainly since what else is there to do without you around to stir up shit?"

She punched him on the arm. "Hey, now, that's not funny. Well, not *particularly* funny."

"I try." He shrugged, then rubbed his arm.

It was late morning, and the day was beautiful. Not fully sunny, but close enough for Oregon. After a cup of strong coffee, Bailey and Roland decided to go into town to speak to people they knew and inform them about what was going on.

Jacob waved a hand. "We'll hold the fort. I need to...ugh, sit here and rest for a while, I think. Yeah..."

Bailey nodded. "No more of Russell's coffee after like, two or three. Get real sleep tonight."

The couple stepped outside and made for Bailey's Camaro.

"So," she said, "days like today are *made* for driving damn nice cars if you ask me."

"Seconded." Roland kissed her on the cheek, and she revved the engine.

They cruised into town, stopping whenever they encountered someone they were close to who would spread the word.

The first person they met was Will Waldsbach, alpha of the South Cliff pack, who'd acted as Bailey's bodyguard and one of her strongest supporters during the fight against the Venatori. He and two of his wolves were hanging out in the front yard of a house Bailey didn't recognize, talking and drinking beer.

"Hey," the werewitch called to them. "Come on over. I got something to tell you guys. Good news, don't worry."

"Bailey!" Grinning, Will ran up. "Things have been pretty boring lately, so hearing that it's *good* news is a little concerning."

She snorted. "Yeah, yeah, enjoy your lack of danger, dumbass."

He and his friends listened as she told them everything. Will had accompanied her into the Weres' sacred temple within the Other, so she didn't hold anything back.

"A goddess," he marveled, running a hand through his hair and beard. "You now sit on some council that, what, rules the world?"

"Not exactly," she clarified, "but we watch over a lot of it. Mostly a good thing, but I'm sure I'll have my work cut out for me."

Then they stopped by the police station to speak to Sheriff Browne and his deputies. In his case, Bailey left out a few of the more esoteric details, though Browne was well aware that the world was full of strange paranormal things.

"What the hell," he rumbled, fingering his mustache and leaning his heavy bulk against the wall. He had mostly recovered the use of his injured leg. "So you now have authority over the, ah, elements that invaded our town multiple times? That's a step in the right direction, if so. Use your position wisely, but don't forget to obey the law when you're in my town."

She laughed. "I won't, Sheriff. Keep up the good work."

Next they went to the diner and spoke to patrons and servers alike as they ordered a light lunch.

Tomi, the usual senior waitress, seemed faintly nervous but optimistic. "I don't claim to understand everything in our universe. It's a big, mysterious place, and scary stuff has gone down here too many times. If you have the power to keep us safe, well, that makes me feel a lot better."

"I do," Bailey affirmed, "and that's gonna be my top priority."

With their meal eaten, they wandered outside and stood in the back lot, thinking about what to do next.

"Vacation?" Roland suggested.

Bailey grimaced. "Shit, I dunno. Might not have time for one. My responsibilities have gone through the roof. If things stay peaceful, I won't be summoned to the council much, but who knows? Still, we have the rest of the day and probably tomorrow."

He put an arm around her, but she jabbed him in the ribs with a finger. "There's something we still need to do. Right away."

Three cars raced down the highway, curving around the eastern Cascade mountains before ascending into the blue peaks. One vehicle was a Camaro, one was an Audi, and one was a Ford Model T.

The Camaro and the Audi were neck and neck near the front, each trying to pass the other while the road was still straight; a curve around a cliff was coming up, and it was too dangerous to attempt a pass there. The Model T chugged along behind them.

Then the Camaro hit a bad bump, swerved, and slowed. The Audi jetted ahead, cutting the other vehicle off the instant they hit the curve.

"*Motherfucker*," Bailey snapped. "He's gonna pay for that."

A convoy of SUVs came down the mountain from the other direction, honking frantically at them for driving so fast even though they were staying in their lanes. Looking into her rearview mirror, Bailey saw Gunney leaning out the side of the Model T and giving them the finger.

She cracked up, then realized she'd made a serious error.

In the time it took her to look back, the road straightened again. The Model T's engine roared, and Gunney shot past her.

"Goddammit!" She punched the dashboard. "I'm a goddess, and I won't be beaten by those scrubs."

She could cheat, but that wouldn't be as much fun as beating them the old-fashioned way.

But the mountains seemed to conspire against her; there wasn't enough road for her to pass both cars, and this time Roland knew the road as well as she did. To both their surprise, though, Gunney managed to force the wizard's car aside and into the shoulder against the railing, then rocketed ahead.

The girl's jaw dropped. "You gotta be kidding me."

The Model T was first to cross the line separating the road from the scenic overlook near the top of the peak. From out the driver's side window, Bailey could hear a faint "*Yeeeeehaw!*"

All three cars came to a stop near the cluster of empty picnic tables, and their drivers emerged.

Gunney brushed his hands against each other. "Not bad

for an old man. I won't lie, though, Seattle Boy almost beat me."

Roland shrugged. "I did better than Bailey, and that's what counts."

Fuming, the girl just waved a finger at them both. They knew her well enough to be perfectly aware that a rematch was forthcoming.

With the fun stuff done, they locked their cars and pulled coolers out of the trunks, assembling a light dinner of sandwiches and cold sodas to eat at the picnic tables on the summit's overlook. No one else was around, and only two cars passed over the course of an hour.

They talked about nothing important, simply enjoying the clear mountain air of the late afternoon.

Bailey heard a distinctive noise behind her and mentally pictured a glowing purple doorway. Heavy footsteps approached as she turned around in her seat.

"Hi, Fenris," she greeted her mentor. "Want some processed meat and cheese on bleached bread with condiments full of preservatives and shit?"

The wolf-father made a sour face. "No, thank you. I will eat later. I came to check in on you. Things are quiet on the council for the time being. They will summon you when they need you."

"Good," she said. "And we're fine. Kinda needed a day off."

He came closer and put a hand on her shoulder. "You've earned it. You have come so far, farther than I could have hoped. I'm proud of you, Bailey."

The girl blushed. "Thank you. You know I get embarrassed by excess praise, though."

"Right," Gunney chimed in. "That's why I stick to insulting her. Seriously, I'm proud of you too, girl. You might be exactly what a council of the gods needs at a time like this."

She shrugged. "We'll see. I'll try my best."

The mechanic continued, "And to think, this all started because I was dumb enough to mention that the sheriff had some out-of-towner—meaning this skinny guy here—at the station and you were curious. Weird."

The girl chortled. "Yeah, and things *really* started when we found out what the problem was." She slapped Roland's chest vaguely, and he pretended to recoil in pain. "Those witches wanted his body for breeding purposes. Of course, no one can claim that right but me these days."

Roland added, "And at a time when you just wanted to evade marriage. Odd, isn't it?"

"Right," she confirmed.

The wizard cleared his throat. "So, that reminds me. With you being an official goddess, does that mean you're out of everyone's league?"

In a quiet voice, she replied, "I hope not."

"Good." Roland stood up, then knelt beside her. "I don't have the necessary accessories to be doing this, but we'll work on that later. Still, I'd rather ask now before I, uh, forget."

She stared at him as Gunney and Fenris watched in silence.

"Roland?" she began.

He spoke before she could ask any questions of her own. "Bailey, will you marry me?"

Her vision spun. She went cold inside, then it turned

into an alternating cascade of cold and warmth, light and dark; too many emotions at once to deal with. She felt like she was melting.

Beside her, Gunney breathed, "Well, I'll be damned."

Bailey jumped up and bear-hugged the wizard, whom she'd wanted to be with practically since the first time they'd spoken. "You dumbass," she said. "Of course I will. What kind of question is that?"

Gunney burst out laughing as they kissed.

"Again," Roland added as their lips parted, "sorry I don't have the ring yet for a *proper* marriage proposal, but we'll deal with that soon."

"Sure," she said. "At least you chose a place with a hell of a view." The mountains were the only witnesses besides the mechanic and the wolf-god.

Shrugging, Roland went on, "I mean, it will be slightly embarrassing, my wife having a better job as a major deity than I do. I'll be left behind in the house, fodder for a show called *Real House-Husbands of I-Can't-Find-This-Town-on-a-Map, Oregon* or something like that. But I'll manage."

She laughed. "Yeah, I'm sure you will."

The four of them passed out the hours of daylight together, talking a little but otherwise content to feel each other's warmth as the sun went down behind the western peaks.

Velasquez smiled. "I gotta admit," he began, "I've never seen this before. I'm looking forward to it, after all the trouble she caused."

He looked down at the silvery canister in his hands, which glowed faintly magenta with the arcane residue of the creature that had once been Caldoria McCluskey.

Beside him stood Park, holding the other canister, which glowed greenish and held her life force. "Yup," he agreed.

The technician who ran the esoteric equipment room came up and reported, "Gentlemen, the dissipator is ready. It's set up to do the arcane aura first. That way, on the off chance that something goes wrong and the entity's life force escapes, it will be powerless, whereas arcane essence escaping can cause all sorts of problems."

"Yes," said Velasquez. "Good."

He and his partner walked over to the piece of equipment, which resembled a silver vending machine with a circular slot at the front, along with an array of buttons and a readout screen. Velasquez inserted his canister and waited for the machine to apprise them of the necessary info.

Both agents blinked.

"What?" Park snapped. "Does that mean it's *missing?*"

The technician, squinting at the screen, stammered, "Uh, yes. If you captured her according to the procedure, and intact, it should say one hundred percent, relative to the size and nature of the entity."

It didn't. According to the readout, only fifty-three percent of an eldritch crone was represented by what was in the canister.

"Bullshit," Velasquez commented. "We followed the procedure exactly and inspected the equipment beforehand to ensure there were no leaks. That means that she wasn't intact when we captured her."

Park quipped, "Well, yeah. She hadn't recovered her full strength, right?"

"Negative," Velasquez elaborated. "But there's more going on, now that I think about it."

"Yes," the technician acceded. "She must have dispersed part of her aura. That's rare, but there is one recorded instance of it happening. You said she was sucking the magic out of random witches to restore herself. Instead of building it all up in her etheric body, she had to have been filtering some of it through her and then sending it out to...I don't know, bolster someone else, maybe?"

Park gritted his teeth. "Goddammit. Why weren't we briefed on that possibility?"

Velasquez thought back to the files he'd read. "Bolstering *several* someone elses," he surmised. "An eldritch crone's arcane aura can infect witches like a pathogen entering the bloodstream. That means she was trying to create other crones, probably to act as her minions. Even if Callie is out of commission, those infectees are out there and in the process of transforming as we speak."

His junior partner stared at him with a mixture of disbelief and faint excitement, while the technician gulped a mouthful of saliva.

"So," Park said, "we're potentially going to have to deal with an army of those things. How much time do we have?"

"Yes, and not much," Velasquez answered him. He turned to the technician. "Finish dissipating this crap for us. We need to talk to the boys, and I'd say a trip to the sub-basement is in order."

The two agents hustled out of the room, picking up the silvery guns they'd used to defeat Callie and making sure they were still charged. Then they made a beeline for the elevator.

It dinged and opened; no one was within. The men entered and stood side by side, disruptor guns held to their chests, their black sunglasses glinting in the harsh white lights of the compartment's interior.

Without looking at his fellow agent, Velasquez mused, "So, you wanted action, Park? Get ready for a shit-ton of it. We've got a new secret war brewing, and it's up to us to stop it before it happens."

"Good deal," Park commented.

The doors closed in their faces, and the elevator descended into darkness.

Fenris was among the few entities who'd ever bothered to come to such a lonely and foreboding corner of the Other. It was a place formed by the magical residues of dying supernatural beings, the etheric emanations of powers spent at the moment when violence faded and gave way to death.

The sky was a deep rust color, and the land resembled a desert in its stony, dusty hardness, yet there were enough trees for a forest, though all were dead or dying, petrified, hollow, diseased, or withered. Pale, sickly grass grew in random patches between the trees, and all the vegetation seemed to be stained with old blood.

Before Fenris was a black reflecting pool similar to ones found elsewhere in the arcane dimension. He sat facing it, looking at nothing in particular as he meditated.

Behind the wolf-father, footsteps approached, and a shadow grew large amidst the dim reddish light. Then a figure stopped beside him, before falling to one knee.

"Fenris," said Carl.

The god addressed the scion without looking at him. "Yes? What is your assessment of the situation?"

Carl smiled grimly. "Balder didn't suspect a thing. He's the god of innocence, after all. He's naturally trusting."

"Good," Fenris replied. "It's said that a man cannot serve two masters, but that does not apply when you are serving *me*. Soon you will inhabit the wasted space Balder currently occupies. Your shapeshifting abilities are perhaps the equal of my own. Thor and Coyote and Thoth will suspect nothing either."

The scion almost trembled with anticipation. "Thank you, wolf-father."

Fenris nodded. He had scooped Carl up long ago, recognizing his potential, then groomed and cultivated him to be an infiltrator among gods. He was Fenris's loyal servant by the time Balder "discovered" him and went through the farce of training him as his disciple.

"And so," the lycanthropic deity went on, "our work will be half done. Three seats emptied of fools. The remaining three will be that much easier to remove afterward."

"Yes," the scion agreed. "How will Bailey fit into the next stage of the plan, now that she sits on the council?"

Fenris paused before he spoke. "The details we will work out as we come to them, but I will find a way—and soon—to set Bailey against the remaining gods while turning them all against one another as well. Divided, they will fall, and if they somehow remain standing, they'll be distracted while we make our moves. We are close, Carl. Very close."

As he conjured a small fire and a stone kettle and cups to go with it, Fenris reflected that even Carl did not know the whole story. The scion thought his mentor's plans ended with taking over all six seats in the crystal chamber and ruling in the pantheon's stead.

The only one who knew that Ragnarök was the final goal was Freya, and she was dead.

"Let us drink, then," Fenris proclaimed as he brewed strong and bitter black tea, "to a better world."

You made it! Here we are at the end of book 7. Thank you so much for reading this far.

Well, hasn't this been a week? More hurricanes, Covid in the highest officials of the land, and earthquakes in Arkansas. What else will this year bring?

For me, it's going to bring an inflatable hot tub, so I have been perusing the "Best Of" articles on the internet. I have it nailed down now, but it will take a while to get the pavers laid to put it on and the electricity to the right place and such.

While I was contemplating getting a hot tub, I remembered visiting some friends years ago in the hills above Sausalito, California. They were house-sitting at a very fancy mansion overlooking the ocean, and they had a side porch with a hot tub off it. The owner fed the raccoons in the area, and my friends had to put dog chow out every night for them. Two in particular came by nightly, and my friends called them Betsy and Gigantor. If they didn't get that chow out by 7pm, Betsy hung off the door handle on the patio and growled. Very disturbing.

How does that lead to hot tubs? Well, we decided to use the house's tub one night, and we went out and checked it during the day. The cover was locked down securely, and there were some golf clubs nearby, which puzzled us. I mean, the cover we understood because animals could push it off. We just figured the owner had left his golf clubs out there.

That night, we discovered their purpose. We went out to watch the Perseid meteor shower from the tub, taking our wine and nibbles. After about ten minutes of getting ourselves settled, we got into some serious meteor-watching.

Then growls came from all sides of us.

What seemed like hundreds of eyes glared at us from the darkness, and three bold raccoons advanced and lunged at us as we sat in the hot tub. The golf clubs were there for brandishing at the raccoons! We had neatly stacked them to one side, but my friend finally got his hands on one (I think it was a nine-iron) and, as he wielded it like a sword in a bad movie to keep them off us, we fled. The next morning, we retrieved the (empty) dishes and glasses. Hope the raccoons liked the wine and cheese!

I always thank my advance readers and the proofreader team, the ones who read my stories after they are edited. They help make this book (and every book) its best. Couldn't do it without you, folks! Much appreciated!

I hope you enjoyed Bailey's and Boland's further adventures. They will be back. And if you get a moment, drop me a review, please. Those are the lifeblood of any writer. We appreciate you!

Until next time,
Renée

Renée Jaggér Social

Website:
https://reneejagger.com/

Facebook Here:
https://www.facebook.com/reneejaggerauthor/